where's molly

a cat & mouse spin-off

USA TODAY BESTSELLING AUTHOR

Cover Design: Opulent Swag & Designs
Art: @tinyhoomanart

First Edition: February 2024

playlist

GABRIELLE CURRENT- B&W
UNDEROATH- ANOTHER LIFE
LITTLE OCEANS- PEACE
STORY OF THE YEAR- A PART OF ME
YUNG'CID & MAXX XERO- ENDLESS
NIGHTMARE
COLORBLIND- GHOSTS
THE USED- MOSH 'N CHURCH
ELLERY BONHAM- SWAY
AMY STROUP- IN THE SHADOWS

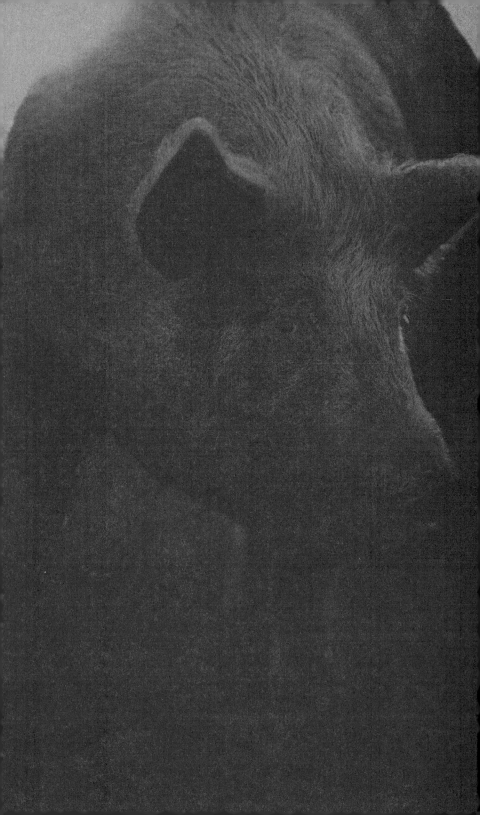

author's note

BEFORE YOU CONTINUE, IT IS **HIGHLY** RECOMMENDED TO READ THE CAT & MOUSE DUET BEFORE READING WHERE'S MOLLY.

READING ORDER:

SATAN'S AFFAIR
HAUNTING ADELINE
HUNTING ADELINE
WHERE'S MOLLY

important note

THIS IS A DARK ROMANCE THAT INCLUDES TRIGGERS SUCH AS MURDER, GORE, GRAPHIC LANGUAGE, GRAPHIC SEXUAL SITUATIONS, CHILD ASSAULT AND RAPE (NOT DEPICTED), TOXIC RELATIONS BETWEEN THE MAIN CHARACTERS, CHILD ABUSE AND NEGLECT, SUICIDAL THOUGHTS AND IDEATIONS, HUMAN TRAFFICKING, DRUG AND ALCOHOL USE, AND ANIMALS BEING FED SUSPECT SHIT (THEY ARE NOT ABUSED, I PROMISE).

THIS BOOK ALSO INCLUDES KINKS SUCH AS BITING, BREATH PLAY, BLOOD PLAY, AND DEGRADATION.

**PLEASE PROCEED WITH CAUTION AND PRIORITIZE YOUR MENTAL HEALTH.
—H. D. CARLTON**

prologue

MOLLY

**PRESENT
2022**

THE LOUD CRUNCH OF blunt teeth biting through bone is a lullaby I could fall asleep to for the rest of my life.

I wrinkle my nose.

The obnoxious sound of lip-smacking that follows is not.

"I can teach you to respect me, but apparently, learning manners is asking too much," I mutter, my upper lip curling in disgust when bloody drool splatters onto the plastic tarp before my worn boots.

Gross.

I'm in my barn, crouched on the outside of their pens, keeping my distance while the five massive pigs eat their dinner. They can very easily grab me through the fence if I dare to get close enough, and that is not an attack I'm likely to survive. They're incredibly strong, and if I do manage to escape, I'll definitely be missing a few limbs.

It makes me wonder why the world is so afraid of a zombie apocalypse, when we're already surrounded by animals more than capable of tearing us apart and devouring every last fucking bit of our flesh and bones.

We're just lucky they haven't figured that out yet. Or rather, they haven't figured out how to escape the prisons we put them in.

When finished, they eagerly sniff the hay, searching for their next piece.

"Last one," I warn them, as if they can even understand me.

Sadly enough, they're the only ones I *can* talk to most days. My human interaction is limited, and this pig farm gets awfully lonely. But it's something I chose for myself.

And I don't fucking regret it.

I toss the rest of the leg at their feet, watching them tear into the severed limb in earnest. Tendons, muscles, and veins shred in a matter of seconds, followed by that satisfying *crunch*.

Right then, my phone in my back pocket buzzes. Sighing, I slide it out and answer without bothering to see who it is. I already know.

"Is it finished?" the female voice asks tonelessly. She's been calling me for the last four years, and I still don't know her name.

"Yup," I answer. "They just ate the last of him."

"Good. We'll contact you when the next subject is due to arrive."

The phone goes dead before I can respond. Not that I would've bothered to—that's always been the extent of our conversations.

My human interaction is *very* limited.

Especially because that's what my pets like to eat for dinner.

"Thanks, Petunia," I chirp to myself. Every time she hangs up, I give her a new name. One day, I'm confident I'll have guessed her real name correctly at least once, though I'd never know.

I have a feeling it's not Petunia, but crazier things have happened.

I double-check that the last of the man I fed to the pigs is completely consumed, and then I start the tedious process of cleaning their pens, my table, and the tools, along with burning his hair and clothes and scattering his powdered teeth in the mountains behind my house. Ensuring every last trace of Carl Forthright is gone.

He who was once a rapist and child trafficker is now pig shit.

So fucking poetic.

"You're lucky I love you little assholes because you guys are fucking *messy*," I complain to the snorting pigs, wrinkling my nose when I spot a chunk of flesh on the floor outside their pen.

They're absolute pains in my ass most days, but I wouldn't trade them for the world.

They keep me sane.

And the devil knows that's hanging on by a goddamn thread.

chapter one

MOLLY

FIFTEEN YEARS AGO
OCTOBER 20TH, 2007

"I'M GONNA HEAD TO the gas station to grab Layla a few things," I tell Dad while frowning at the mess in the living room.

Five crushed, empty beer cans are scattered on the end table, along with empty chip bags and dip with the lid left open.

My father is anxiously peering out of the tattered curtains, shirtless, his pot belly bulging out over his jeans. His gray hair is balding on top, and despite his stomach, he's a tall, lanky old man with a defined jaw, eyebrows that are constantly furrowed, and wrinkles covering every inch of his face.

"No, I need you here. You've been gone all damn day," he snaps, hardly sparing me a glance.

It's after eight-thirty at night, and I've been waitressing at the diner all day. I'm exhausted, but for what feels like the millionth time, she's out of diapers and no one mentioned it. I'm turning twenty tomorrow, but I'll have to pick up another shift now that I'm spending today's tip money on Layla.

"She needs her diaper changed, and there isn't any more," I argue.

He snarls, letting the curtain fall as he faces me.

"She ain't none of your concern."

But she is.

She's sure as fuck not *his* concern, even though she's his daughter.

Dad scratches his arm, track marks blemishing his skin. Again, he glances toward the curtains, as if he's waiting for someone to show up. Probably one of his creepy friends, sure to arrive with a book bag full of drugs, despite the fact that he just made me buy him some yesterday.

"I won't be longer than twenty minutes," I reason. "I just need diapers and formula."

Anxiety spikes in my chest as Layla begins to cry from upstairs. I just laid her down, and I had hoped she'd stay asleep until I got back. She's been fussy for the past week. Right when her eyes close and I think she's finally asleep, they pop right back open and she releases a sorrowful wail that rips my heart out.

"Let me get Layla settled first, and I'll—"

"No," he barks. "If you're going to go, then go now. I ain't got all fucking night."

"Fine," I mumble.

My four-month-old sister is now screaming at the top of her lungs, while our mother is knocked out on the couch, her mouth open and drool trailing down her chin as she softly snores.

A used needle lies on the coffee table in front of her, a bead of blood still staining the tip.

She won't be waking up, which means that Layla will be left to her tears while I'm gone.

Sighing, I head toward the door, pausing briefly when I hear Dad call out, "And grab me a pack of cigs and another six-pack of beer!"

I don't bother answering—not that he expects one. He knows I'll do what he says. If I don't, I'll have to invest in another bottle of concealer. The one I have is almost empty.

The sound of Layla's screams is silenced as I shut the door behind me, my anxiety worsening and gnawing at my stomach. Her poor little throat will be sore, and I'm sure her head will be hurting by the time I get back.

She hates it when I leave her alone, and *I* hate what that implies. There are days that I wonder if it's more than just an attachment to me that puts that fear in her eyes when I walk away.

If Dad is hurting her like he hurt me...

I don't know what I'll do. Except when I'm finished, I'll be covered in blood.

My hands tremble as I speed-walk to the gas station a few blocks down the road. It's a warm and breezy fall night in October—likely one of our last before winter approaches.

Reaper Canyon, Montana, is surrounded by the Electric Peak range, and it's where I was born and raised. The daunting name of this small town is fitting, considering it's where everyone's dreams go to die. This state exudes beauty, but even the mountains off in the distance can't take away the ugliness of my world.

I keep my head down, focusing on the hole in the tip of my dirty tennis shoes. My feet are too big for them now, but I haven't had the money to get a new pair yet. All of it goes to Layla or buying my parents drugs.

On my sixteenth birthday, Dad threatened to kick me out of the house if I didn't get a job. Said I needed to start pulling my weight around the house, as if going to school, doing all the chores, and getting their drugs for them wasn't enough. Let alone being at his and Mom's beck and call twenty-four seven.

My entire first paycheck went on their cigarettes, beer, and drugs. Now, they rely on me to buy our food, and everything for Layla.

The overhead bell chimes as I walk into the local gas station, drawing the clerk's attention. Aside from Layla, he's the only person in this world I actually like.

"Hey, Mol," he greets, a smile stretching across his face, laugh lines forming in his brown skin. He's one of the few people I know who is always happy. I don't believe I've ever known that feeling. Maybe when Layla smiled at me for the first time. But it was fleeting. It didn't take long for my parents to steal away the joy again.

"Hi, Mario," I return, waving at him before disappearing down one of the aisles and heading straight for the coolers where the beer is held.

I'm not old enough to buy alcohol, but Mario now knows my dad well enough to understand that if I don't bring it home, I'll show up with bruises on my face the next day, pleading for him to let me buy it. He's tried to call the police, but each time, I get on my knees and beg him not to. I didn't want to risk Layla being taken by CPS and put in the system.

Families love young girls to adopt, but so do predators, and I won't take the risk. At least at home, I can protect her.

So, despite Mario's hatred for my parents, he risks his license and sells me the alcohol, seeing as he knows it's not for me anyway. He's already made me pinkie swear to wait to drink until I'm old enough, though he told me to stay away from cigarettes forever.

I readily agreed. I've seen addiction in my mother, who, at one point, was valedictorian and had a full ride to college. But then she met my father, and all those dreams and aspirations didn't seem to matter so much when she had euphoria coursing through her veins.

I grab Dad's favorite beer, diapers and formula for Layla, and a few packs of ramen for the next couple days.

Dropping the items on the counter, I pull out my cash while Mario turns to get a pack of cigarettes from behind him. Dad's favorite.

"How are you tonight, sweetheart?" he asks me, clicking the keyboard to ring everything up.

I sigh. "Same ol', same ol'."

"Dad still giving you trouble?"

I give him a dry glance. "Always. I'll be spending my birthday at the diner tomorrow. I was supposed to have the day off, but I didn't get good tips today and, well—" I wiggle the measly bundle of cash. "—it's all gone now anyway."

Mario shoots me an unimpressed look. "What's stopping you from taking Layla from them?"

Shame prevents me from meeting his eyes.

This isn't the first time he's asked, but every excuse I've come up with falls flat. Because the truth is condemning, and as much as I like Mario, what if I can't trust him?

When I refocus on him, my heart squeezes. His stare is soft, and he radiates genuine concern. I feel my resolve cracking.

"Please, Mol, you can tell me anything."

I sigh, and the last of my reservations crumble at his feet.

"My parents have proof of me buying drugs—*their* drugs—but it doesn't matter. It looks bad. They know I want her, and they've threatened to show it to the court if I try to take custody. Dad has pictures and videos I didn't even know he was taking, but he showed me them before he hid them. And if I just take her... I'll be kidnapping her. I'm legally an adult, but the moment I found out my mother was pregnant, I got comfortable in my prison. I can't leave her, Mario."

My friend shakes his head, utter disgust emitting from his brown eyes. "They're sick. Sick, sick people. And they're blackmailing you! Maybe a lawyer—"

"Lawyers cost money, Mario. Money that I *don't* have. All of it goes to them, and I..." My words fail me, helplessness taking root. Exhaling harshly, I finish with the only words that matter, "I'm trapped."

Tears burn the backs of my eyes as Mario stares at me with fury. Fury *for* me, I know. But his anger won't change my situation.

I don't even know how to.

"You don't have any other family?" he questions, the hope hanging on to his words brittle.

Frowning, I shake my head. As far as I know, both of my parents are only children, and their parents are either dead or estranged.

I have no one but Layla.

"I can ask my wife and see about you staying with us—"

I'm shaking my head before he can finish. "My parents won't let me take Layla, and I can't leave her alone."

"Molly, *please* let me help you," Mario begs. "We can figure something out."

"I need time," I snap, and he deflates. Guilt rises, and it only cements my helplessness. "Just... I'll figure it out eventually, okay? She's so young right now, so I just need to make sure I go about it the right way."

He nods, relenting, though his stiff movements betray his true feelings. But just like me, he's helpless.

Even if I take my parents down, they'll be sure to bring me down with them.

"Then at least let me pay for Layla's stuff, yeah? I'll help you get anything she needs in the meantime. But don't think I'm not going to find you a way out of this, little girl," he tells me sternly. "I won't ever stand idly by while you suffer."

Tears well in my eyes, and I'm too overwhelmed with gratitude to thank him properly.

Eventually, I choke out, "Thank you. Even if I have no other family, at least I have you."

His shoulders slump, though the conviction in his tone is strong. "You do, sweetheart. For anything."

I smile softly, even if it's hard to feel. But I am eternally grateful for him, especially since he's the only person who's ever been kind to me.

The bell chimes, and I glance at the newcomers walking in. Quickly, I do a double take, a frown marring my face.

It's my dad, along with a man I don't recognize. I'd have thought they were two strangers who walked in at the same time if it wasn't for them being in the midst of a hushed conversation, their words halting when they finally catch sight of me.

My heart drops.

"What are you doing here? I'm getting your stuff..." I ask, trailing off with nervousness when I realize the other man is staring at me with an expression I can't quite describe. It's a look I don't *want* to decipher, with how it immediately has the hairs on the back of my neck standing on end.

He's short and stocky, with trimmed hair and a square, pronounced jawline. His pale skin is covered in shitty tattoos, and there's a cold gleam in his brown eyes.

Dad strides toward me, gesturing for me to move aside. "I'll take that off your hands. You're too young to be buying alcohol anyhow. Why don't you go with my friend here and wait for me till I'm done?" he orders gruffly.

My mouth drops, bewildered and increasingly suspicious.

My dad has *never* come to take anything 'off my hands'. Which means there's a reason he's here, and that terrifying man has something to do with it.

Like hell I'm going anywhere with him.

"It's fine, I got it—"

"Go," he barks. "*Now.*"

My spine snaps straight. It isn't the harshness in his voice that has me on edge, but rather, the urgency.

Dumbfounded, I look to Mario, and find him a lip curl away from all-out snarling at my dad. He's glaring at the two men with distrust and wrath that burn hotter than the underworld beneath our feet. But what can he do? If he calls the police and accuses me of trying to buy beer just to get me away from them, I would still end up going home with Dad later, and Mario could get his license revoked if they find out he's sold to me before. And if he claims Dad's a threat to me, it'll only separate me from Layla.

I could run... But where would I go? I couldn't leave my four-month-old sister alone, nor did I have anywhere safe to take her.

My mind is spinning over different scenarios, but each time, I come to the same conclusion. I'm helpless.

"I've actually been needing some help around this place. Why doesn't she stay here with me, and I'll pay—"

"You got eyes for my daughter or somethin', buddy? Why don't you mind your own goddamn business, huh?" Dad snaps, glaring at Mario.

"It's fine," I whisper, glancing at the strange man nervously. He's still staring at me, sending a cold shiver down my spine. Whoever he is, he's the reaper, and wherever he takes me, I won't be going anywhere but down.

"Go with him, Molly. I'm not gonna tell you again," Dad barks.

Working to swallow, I hesitantly step away from the counter. Sparing Mario one last glance, I tuck my chin down and walk toward the man, adrenaline releasing into my veins with an intensity I've never felt before. My pulse is thundering in my ears, and I'm beginning to feel nauseous.

A wicked smile curls one side of the stranger's lips, and my stomach fills with acid, bile teasing the bottom of my throat.

"Your dad and I are good friends, don't worry," he assures, grinning wider as if that's supposed to ease my nerves.

It feels as if there is glue on the bottom of my feet, making each step difficult as we head toward the door.

I can't do this. I can't just let this man take me so easily. Wherever I'm going, I won't go without a fight.

I'll take Layla and find somewhere for us to go. Because wherever that is, it *has* to be better than where we are now. Even if I'm a fucking fugitive wanted for kidnapping, I'll find a way for us to survive.

Just as the man opens the door, the bell chiming, I take off down the aisle to my right.

"Hey!" Dad shouts, prompting his friend to whip around. He wastes no time charging after me, causing my heart to jump in my throat.

Instinctively, I grab a few items from the shelves and throw them on the ground behind me. Bags of chips, granola bars, and other foods scatter across the dirty tile, but it doesn't deter him. He jumps over them, his finger skating across my shoulder as I round a corner, only to find my dad standing right there. I scream, nearly smacking directly into his chest.

His arms come up to wrap around me, so I duck below him, scarcely evading them. I just manage to squeeze past him, hearing their muttered curses from behind me.

"Goddammit, you little bitch!" Dad spits.

Heart pounding viciously against my rib cage, I dart down another aisle, seeing Mario come into view. He's holding a baseball bat while speaking frantically on the phone with people who I assume are the police.

"Get here now!" Mario shouts over the phone.

I send more items flying to the ground. This time, it's bottles of soda, all bouncing on the ground, causing some of them to pop open or completely explode.

Quickly, I glance over my shoulder just as the two men stop short of the spillage. I catch sight of the demonic look passing over my father's face. And I know that whatever they have planned for me, it'll make my home life seem like Candy Land.

They split up, Dad going in one direction and the man running to the opposite aisle. They're going to trap me.

Panic invades my senses, and I attempt to backtrack and climb over one of the shelves. The man rounds the corner and charges toward me.

I'm determined to keep going, until I see him reach into the back of his jeans in my peripheral, followed by a distinct click.

I freeze, hanging halfway on the shelf with ice running through my veins, then peer over my shoulder.

Mario is now staring down the barrel of a gun, his face frozen in terror while the man holds it steadily. His face is twisted in anger as he pants heavily.

"I will fucking shoot him. You really want that death on your hands, little girl?" the man hisses.

A thunderous expression is on Dad's face as he stomps toward me, pointing toward the back door labeled for employees only.

"Let's go. Right fucking now!"

I have no choice but to listen.

There's no more running.

I had an opportunity but couldn't get to the exit in time. And as tempted as I am to keep fighting, I won't risk Mario's life.

Panting, and tears blurring my vision, I climb down from the shelf and head toward the door. As I pass Mario, I wave, whispering the word, "Bye," before heading toward the door.

With a deep breath, I walk through the stockroom and out of the back exit. I follow the man through the back alley, my dad breathing down my neck as we walk. There, I'm surrounded by three more men.

There's no chance to scream. Not as they grip my biceps, slap a cloth over my mouth, and drag me into their black van.

It's over for me. I'll never get to see Layla again.

Even worse, she'll never see me again—the only person who took care of her—kept her *safe*.

The only question I have is, will her fate be worse, or mine?

chapter two

MOLLY

FOURTEEN YEARS AGO
JUNE 18TH, 2008

I READ OVER THE last word I wrote on the page before snapping the journal shut. It's a diary I've been secretly writing in for the past couple weeks. It's been my only form of release, but I refuse to take it with me, even if it was the only thing that kept my detonating sanity somewhat intact. It's the only outlet I had for my pent-up rage.

And it can burn with the rest of this house, for all I care.

I hope to God another girl never finds this journal. That would mean she replaced me, and no one—*no one*—should ever have to experience the horrors of this house. No one innocent, at least. I wouldn't care if Francesca, Rocco, or any of his friends got a taste of their own poison one day. It's the least they fucking deserve.

My broken heart is pounding heavily against my chest, the jagged pieces cutting up the inside with each beat. However, the adrenaline coursing through my veins mutes the pain. The only thing I can feel is determination and fury. So much fucking fury.

I'm not waiting any longer. *I can't.*

Francesca has something planned for us in two days, and while I suspect we'll be auctioned off, she never said.

All I know—I can't be here when it happens.

Another day in this hellhole, and I'll lose my fucking mind. Another day without Layla, and I'll kill anyone I have to, even if it ends in my own death. It'll only be my body that dies, anyway. They've already destroyed my soul, and all that's left is an empty house that has seen as many tragedies as the one I'm planning to escape tonight.

My pulse thuds in my ears as I quietly slide out of my bed and tiptoe to the hole beneath the floorboard. When I first arrived here, I noticed the panel was loose, and after a week's effort, I finally managed to pry it up. It was just a dirty hole, but now it's the home of all my secrets and heartache.

With trembling hands, I set the journal inside, carelessly dropping the pen in after it. Then, I slide the wooden piece back into place.

There's no clock in here, but Rocco and his friends have quieted completely, which means they likely passed out. According to Francesca and her constant complaining, that typically happens around two or three AM every night.

I've been preparing for this for *months.*

And now that it's finally here, I'm terrified I missed something. A small detail I didn't plan for when I've done nothing *but* plan.

The only thing separating me from freedom are these thin walls and miles and miles of woods.

That, and the guard stationed outside the house. I've stayed up from dusk to dawn several nights to watch him, forgoing precious sleep to learn his schedule and habits. Which often led me to getting in trouble for falling asleep during lessons. Though Francesca has long since grown tired of my disobedience, she won't get rid of me either.

I'm one of four who made it through the Culling—a twisted game a group of pedophiles and rapists created for sport. The objective is to put us in the woods filled with traps, where they'll hunt us with crossbows. If we're hit, we're punished. If we win and outrun them, we're considered superior meat and then put up for auction.

It's an insult to kidnap us only to make us prove ourselves worthy of being kidnapped.

It makes no fucking sense and was only created so bored rich people can be less bored.

They'll never get the fucking chance.

Inhaling a deep breath, I creep toward my bedroom door. The crickets chirp loudly from outside my window, as if they're cheering me on. Rooting for a precarious escape. One that is likely to kill me.

But I'd rather die rebelling than die submitting.

Sweat forms along my brow as I slowly turn the rusty knob, cringing when it squeals. I swear to God, this house was built when the dinosaurs roamed and is filthier than Francesca's sins.

The hinges creak, though it doesn't stop me from swinging open the door. There are three other girls sleeping in their respective rooms. There's a chance that if one of them catches me, they'll alert Francesca. But I've long since accepted that I'll kill anyone who gets in my way.

No one will keep me from Layla.

My heart races, gaining momentum and slamming against the inside of my chest as I sneak down the long hallway. Aside from my own pulse, it's dead silent. And fuck, is it creepy.

It's always felt haunted here, yet I was convinced it was by the living. Now, I'm not so sure. Or maybe our sadness is potent, even in our dreams.

I bite my lip, holding my breath while I make my way down the steps, avoiding every soft spot in the wood that creaks. The first thing my eyes gravitate to is the green neon numbers blaring from the stove.

2:30 AM. *Perfect.*

Moonlight spears through the kitchen window, but I don't bother with anything in here. I've learned to go days without food and water. But I don't plan on depriving myself for long, seeing as I'm confident there's a town nearby.

Francesca's favorite helper, Rio, makes weekly trips to the grocery store, only gone for a few hours before he returns, and they certainly don't buy in bulk. There has to be a place I can run to and call for help.

I peek into the living room, finding several men laid out over the couch and floor. Five of them. All snoring and surely doped up on drugs, their veins as clogged with chemicals as the dust in the air vents. Their organs are probably floating in an ocean of alcohol, too, pruning in the toxins.

An earthquake would sooner rock them further into whatever depraved la-la land they wandered into than wake them. I wonder, when pedophiles dream of marrying women their age or walking an old person across the street out of the goodness of their hearts, do they call them nightmares? Do they awake in a cold sweat and with a pit of dread in their stomachs?

Surely, they don't consider dreams of cute puppies and rainbows *pleasant.*

Regardless, they're the least of my concerns as I slink through the darkened living room, stepping over stray limbs and crushed, empty beer cans.

It's the guard standing outside the house who has a trail of sweat leaking down my spine.

He would better serve as a boulder in the Hoover Dam with how ossified the muscles around his bones are. All those people that built it died for nothing when all that dumb fuck needed to do was just fucking *stand there.*

But if he sticks to the routine he's followed for the last three months, then he should be holding his dick in the woods somewhere, taking a piss break. Typically, he combines it with a smoke break, using it as an excuse to walk around and relieve himself from standing in the same position for hours on end.

Maybe he wouldn't fare so well in the dam.

Holding my breath, I grab the handle with a trembling, sweaty palm and crack open the door, the rusted hinges screaming.

Wincing, I peek over my shoulder, quickly ensuring the men behind me are still unconscious, then slip out the door.

Only to smack directly into a hard chest.

"Where ya goin', mama?"

Hope, elation, freedom... they fizzle out like a damp firecracker. My bottom lip trembles as I lift my gaze.

Rio.

He wasn't supposed to be on duty tonight.

He's tall, and his light brown skin is covered in tattoos. His hair is buzzed close to his scalp, accentuating a strong jawline and full lips. Admittedly, he's incredibly enigmatic, and the only man in this house who doesn't make us recoil in fear.

He's never been interested in any of us.

Francesca brought him in a few months ago, right after his nineteenth birthday, and not long after he arrived from Puerto Rico. She joked she didn't feel so bad hiring a kid when he's old enough to fuck. I don't think that vile woman is capable of shame or guilt, nor does she pretend to be when she calls him into her bedroom at night.

Just like ours, his eyes are haunted. And unlike the other men, he doesn't leer at the girls or smile when we're raped. In fact, he looks downright sick when it happens.

His job is extraction—a fancy, bullshit name for a kidnapper. They provide him with a picture of a pretty young girl, her name, and her location; his only job is to lure her into his car and bring her back. Most of them are sex workers. Easy to get in a car, and very few people go looking for them once they're missing.

However, they've been having issues with him letting targeted girls slip through his fingers. A mistake that would typically get him killed, but every time Rocco threatens to, Francesca stops him.

She's attached, and it's the only reason Rio is still alive.

I open my mouth, but the answer gets clogged in my throat. It feels too tight, like a crowded room with bystanders pressed shoulder to shoulder, preventing me from uttering a word and wrapping a noose around my neck *and* theirs.

"I got all night. Don't know if you do, though," he drawls casually, pushing for an answer.

"Out," I squeak, the lone syllable forcing its way through the crowd.

A stupid thing to say, but what possible excuse could I conjure? Under no circumstances are we allowed out of our rooms after bedtime, let alone out of the *house*.

I'm fucked. Well and truly fucked.

"Out," he repeats tonelessly.

Adrenaline pumps through my veins, and sweat gathers at the base of my spine. I have the urge to vomit all over his boots, nausea swirling in the pit of my stomach.

I try to clear my throat but only end up squeaking out a choked cough. After tossing a nervous glance over my shoulder, and then over Rio's, I meet his penetrating gaze again.

I'm no longer confident the men behind me won't wake up to our voices, and the guard can show up any second. The smart thing to do is offer him whatever he wants in exchange for his silence and to return to my room. Except something keeps me rooted to where I stand.

Hope.

Hope is what keeps me in place.

He let others go. Maybe he'll let me go, too.

"I'm sorry," I whisper. "I-I'm dying."

I wasn't planning on saying the last part, but it's the truth.

Every second spent in this place—subjected to these waking nightmares—is one less beat my heart is willing to give.

"We all are, no?" he retorts.

I flick another nervous glance over my shoulder. Surprisingly, he takes a step back, allowing me just enough room to step out of the entrance and softly close the door behind me.

A small mercy, yet it means everything to me in this instance.

The warm June air feels like a suffocating blanket at this moment.

"P-please. I'll do anything. I won't tell anyone about this place. About you."

He quirks a brow.

"Is that supposed to convince me? You won't have the option to tell anyone shit if I don't let you go, *estúpida*. And keeping you here means no risk," he hisses quietly, his accent deepening with annoyance.

"Right. That was stupid. But it is still completely the case. I just... I have a sister. She's only a year old, and all alone..." I trail off, realizing I'm telling a sex trafficker that my little sister is super fucking kidnappable.

Stupid. Fucking. *Idiot.*

His other brow joins the first halfway up his forehead.

"You're terrible at this," he comments dryly.

"She's not completely alone," I amend weakly. Then, I sigh impatiently. "Okay, whatever. Telling you that doesn't put her in any more danger than she's already in. My parents are addicts and will have friends come over who tend to go exploring the house at night. I guess the only difference between here and there—I'll be able to kill the sick fuck who touches her if she's with me."

He grins, but I've no idea what the fuck he could possibly find funny.

"If you're lucky, you'll manage to kill one before one of them kills you. Then your sister would *really* be alone."

I growl under my breath. Of course, he's right, but my goal was to tug at his heartstrings, not bring out his logic and reasoning.

Hell, I really do suck at this.

I chew my lip mercilessly, trying to figure out a different angle. The man may be fucked up, but he's proven to have empathy. Somewhere beyond the spiderwebs, venomous snakes, and flesh-eating parasites in his soul is a soft spot. I just have to find it.

Worrying my lip harder, I peek over his shoulder again. I'm running out of time. It's a miracle the others haven't returned yet.

"Do you have a sister?" I ask.

His expression wasn't exactly... expressive to begin with, yet it seems as if his face falls anyway. A dark, ominous look passes over his eyes, and his features sharpen. It sends chills down my spine and the hairs on the back of my neck rise.

I'm not sure if I found the soft spot or just struck a *very* sensitive nerve.

The blood in my body turns to ice. If I hadn't been standing in front of a beast before, I certainly am now.

"Is she alive?" I push.

What's stopping me? I'm dead, anyway.

"Yes," he clips. "But letting you go could get her killed if they decide to retaliate against me."

"They'll never know you saw me," I reason, growing desperate. "You weren't even supposed to be on duty tonight."

He considers that for a moment, and my anxiety amps up.

"Look, we're both desperate to keep our sisters safe, yeah? I don't need to be someone who gets in your way, nor do you need to be for me."

His upper lip curls into a snarl, frustration pinching his brow.

It feels like an eternity passes before he finally speaks again.

"Get out of my face. Now. I sure as fuck hope you know what you're doing, because I'm not helping you, nor will I save you if you're caught."

Relief explodes in my chest, stealing my breath away.

"Thank you. I won't forget you, Rio."

I don't wait for him to respond. With one last glance, I take off down the steps and toward the only place that offers a chance of survival—the unwelcoming arms of the forest.

It will be unkind, but I've suffered much worse.

chapter three

CAGE

PRESENT
2022

"Don't let the job title deter you, man. She may be a pig farmer, but she's fucking hot as hell," Eli says from the other end of the phone. "I'll admit, she's showed up in a few of my fantasies when I—"

"Finish that sentence, and I'll drive off the fucking road," I growl, curling my lip in disgust.

As if I give a fuck about who the dickhead jacks off to. I'll sooner cut off his dick before I listen to him talk about what he does to it.

"I'm just sayin', man. Sexy as fuck."

"Noted," I respond tonelessly.

Don't really give a fuck what she looks like, either. The only thing I'm concerned with is dropping off the two dead assholes in my trunk.

Eli's the one who normally takes care of the drops, until he went and got himself shot in the side. Now, he's on bed rest for six weeks, and I was hired to fill in until he recovers.

I'm no stranger to making criminals disappear, though my methods tend to be very different. And less... messy.

"I'll let Legion know when the job's done. Rest up and leave your goddamn dick alone. I don't want to be hauling around dead bodies longer than I need to," I grumble, then click off the phone. The line goes dead, finally giving me some peace and fucking quiet.

His response wasn't important, anyway.

The moon guides me down the barren dirt road, my headlights switched off. While this pig farmer supposedly doesn't have a neighbor for miles, I still like to take extra precautions.

My job relies on my ability to cover my bases, and I certainly won't sacrifice that now when there are two corpses rotting in my car.

After a few more minutes, I arrive at a lone ranch house nestled beside a massive barn, sitting on over a hundred acres of land. At the entrance of the driveway is an old sign that reads *Paladin Farm*.

The corner of my lip quirks as I recall what *'paladin'* means. How noble.

There's a light shining through a single window from her house and a soft glow emitting from the barn. Otherwise, it's pitch-black out here, allowing an unobstructed view of the Milky Way and its star systems.

I stop by the barn just as a shadowed figure emerges from its depths. She stands at the entrance, hands on her hips as she watches me approach.

Legion warned her that I was coming in Eli's place, yet based on the stiff set of her shoulders and her tapping foot, she's on edge.

Rightfully so.

The minute I step out of my car, I'm greeted with the chilly March breeze and her smooth, angelic voice.

"You're here for the delivery?"

My heart pauses, and a distinct part of my brain is blaring an alarm. I've heard thousands of women's voices over the years, but *that* voice—I swear it's familiar.

"Last time I checked," I return dryly, narrowing my eyes to see her better, and failing.

She hums, clearly unimpressed with my answer.

"Two bodies in the trunk," I inform.

"Bring 'em in," she clips, before pivoting and disappearing into the barn.

Digging in my pocket, I pull out a pack of nicotine gum and pop one in my mouth. Then, I open the trunk, curling my lip at the abhorrent smell that wafts from within.

They're already beginning to bloat.

I carry the first body in the barn, the aroma from the pigs no better. It's much bigger on the inside with smooth concrete flooring. Three pens are to my right, with five large, fat pigs dispersed between them. On the other side is the woman, her back to me as she dresses head to toe in a bright yellow hazmat suit.

Without looking back, she points to an expansive metal table with hair clippers, a large metal contraption with a few buttons, pliers, and a Sawzall laying atop it. "Lay them right there."

I do as she says while she begins slipping on oversized rubber gloves that reach up to her elbows.

"I'm going to grab the other one," I say, regarding her closely.

She's reserved, and though she doesn't watch me with her eyes, I can sense that she knows exactly where I am, aware of every movement I make.

A bead of sweat forms on my brow as I carry in the second man, dropping him on the table next to the other.

Thick, opaque plastic covers the wall in front of her setup, descending to the floor, then across it, reaching the pens.

Seems she also likes to cover her bases.

Protective glasses rim her eyes as she grabs the hair clippers. She won't look directly at me, and a few strands of dark brown curly hair frame her face and hide her features, preventing me from getting a good look at her.

"I got it from here," she says woodenly.

I don't answer, too intent on staring at her to see if my hunch is right.

She sighs, and finally turns to look at me, stealing my breath. Even beneath the large protective glasses, I recognize her immediately. There's no mistaking that fucking scar.

She has big emerald green eyes, a gap below her irises that's always given her a naturally seductive stare. And right below the right one is a permanent white, slightly raised bite mark. A full mouth of teeth scarred into her olive skin. How she got it—I still don't know. But it's evident it's not a pretty story.

She's older but doesn't look much different, only more mature. However, the light brown freckles that are smattered across her cheeks and the button nose soften her features. Nine years ago, I told myself I'd count them, but I never got the chance to finish.

I intend to remedy that.

Her eyes widen, recognition flashing within them. She stumbles back, dropping the hair clippers on the table before bumping into it, evoking a god-awful sound from the metal legs grinding against the floor. Even now, she still resembles a frightened cat.

"Cage? What are you doing here?" she snaps, then urgently peers around me as if I were hiding a whole other person up my ass.

"Making a drop," I answer slowly, my brow pinching with confusion. "You're supposed to be living in Alaska. I put you in Alaska." My tone is accusatory, but I'm pissed.

The lengths I go through to make people disappear are fucking tedious as hell. It feels like a slap in the face to have a person I killed standing right in front of me—*not* in Alaska.

That's not why you're angry.

The intrusive voice in my head can go fuck itself.

She glances around nervously. "I didn't like it there."

The muscle in my jaw tics. "What are you doing here, Molly?"

She rears back, as if I backhanded her across the cheek.

"That's not my name anymore."

"This isn't supposed to be your state of residence either, yet here we are."

She narrows her eyes, fire unleashing within the depths of her irises. "Why do you care? I hired you for a job. You did the job. What I do is no longer your concern."

She's right.

If any other client I made disappear were to materialize in front of me, I'd tell them it'll cost triple to make them disappear a second time. But whatever happens to them in the meantime isn't my fucking problem.

Except, Molly isn't like the other clients I've had.

Mainly because I fucked her thoroughly before I gave her a brand-new identity. Then, she disappeared on me—just like she was supposed to.

And it fucking enraged me.

Now, she stares at me like a tiny rabbit caught in a trap, squealing to be freed.

She escaped me once, and I let her.

I won't allow it a second time.

chapter four

MOLLY

PRESENT
2022

I'm going to kill Legion.

He never told me *Cage* was delivering the bodies. I didn't even think to ask who was coming when I was informed Eli was shot and would have a temporary replacement. I trust Legion implicitly, so I wasn't concerned with their identity. Especially because I know how to protect myself regardless of who it is.

I've no idea if Legion even knows anything about the night I spent with Cage—and maybe he doesn't. But, fuck, he could've warned me.

"When did you come back?" Cage questions, his voice tight.

"Four years ago," I answer automatically, though I'm not sure why. It's none of his business—*I'm* none of his business.

"Why?" he demands.

"Doesn't matter why. You shouldn't be here," I mumble, nervous sweat dotting my hairline and coating my trembling palms. *I* shouldn't be here. We both know that, even if he doesn't know why.

Running from Francesca and Rocco was one of the many reasons I needed to escape Montana. Yet, I knew coming back here was the only thing that would save me from myself.

I tried to survive in Alaska, but only found myself dying.

At least here, I'd be living, even if I still feel dead inside.

Cage takes a step toward me, a savage expression mapped across his devastatingly beautiful face.

I forgot how tall he was. Towering over six-four, at least.

His hair hasn't changed since I last saw him. Still buzzed short on the sides, the dark brown strands only slightly longer on top. *Just* long enough to run my hands through. I recall my tongue tracing his sharp jawline made out of steel and thick brows creased in bliss above his forest green eyes. And I'll never forget those wide, full lips that kissed every inch of my skin, or the light stubble that sent chills down my spine every time I felt it brush against me. All features that my stare has worshiped for hours.

Letting him fuck me was one of many mistakes, but I wanted to feel what everyone else was feeling when they had sex—what normal people felt. I wanted sex to feel *good*.

I just never expected it to feel *that* good. And for unknown reasons, that's still more terrifying than being gang-raped by Rocco and his men.

He takes another step toward me. For the second time, I stumble back into the table where two corpses continue to rot.

"D-don't," I choke out, holding up my hand to stop him. As if it would.

He pauses, the gears in his head turning. I've no idea what he's thinking, but in the short time I knew him, he wasn't very susceptible to letting people inside his head.

"Feed the pigs, Molly," he finally grits out, taking several steps back. I feel the constriction around my chest release with every inch that grows between us.

It's been nine years since I last saw him, though I recall all too well how hard he made it to breathe.

I clear my throat as if that's going to remove the anxiety clogging it. Then, I stiffly turn to the first corpse on the table.

A man who is well into his fifties, with a deeply receded hairline and gray hair. After some maneuvering, I manage to remove the articles of clothing from his body and toss them to the side. Then, I grab the hair clippers again and begin shaving his head.

All the while, Cage watches me silently.

Eli doesn't typically stick around after the deliveries. Not since the first time he watched my pigs eat. I'm tempted to tell Cage to leave, but whatever old attachment I had with him isn't entirely gone. Like removing a Band-Aid and being left with the residue. The wounds are healed, yet what was supposed to help close them remains.

"What did this guy do?" I ask, my voice strained.

"He was just acquitted of raping his fifteen-year-old grandson. Not enough evidence, the judge said. Despite the mountain of pictures of bruises around the kid's neck that matched the guy's handprints and the semen sample on the boy's shorts."

"Sounds like the judge should've been killed, too," I mutter snidely, then grab my pliers and begin forcefully yanking out his teeth. When I'm finished, I drop them in the grinder on my table. With the press of a button, it grinds them down to powder, making them easy to dispose of later.

Next, I turn on the Sawzall and begin cutting into flesh. Crimson splatters onto my gloved hands, face, and chest. Behind me, I hear my pigs snorting loudly beneath the ear-piercing sound of the saw cutting through bone.

Now that they have a steady diet of human remains, they tend to get rowdy once they catch a whiff of blood. It used to freak me out, but then I decided that the predators they were eating were far worse than the beasts consuming them.

After I'm done, his arms, legs, and head are removed from his torso. I move the body parts out of the way, then sweep my arm across the table, wiping the excess blood onto the plastic-covered floor for easy cleanup later.

"And this one?" I ask tersely, breaking the tense silence while I remove the clothing from the second man. He appears well into his seventies, covered in liver spots.

"That's the judge."

I purse my lips, feeling, rather than seeing, his amusement.

"Did you kill them?" I question, realizing that in the nine years I've been gone, a lot could have changed with Cage.

"No. Legion handles that."

Legion is an underground organization run by an elusive no-face man named after his company, who employs hitmen to take out whoever they deem necessary. They specifically target those who

35

frequent the dark web, and much like their sister organization, *Z*, they go after pedophiles.

While *Z* focuses on the trafficking rings and larger operations, *Legion* was formed to focus on the smaller fish—the psychopaths who lurk in plain sight, fitting into society as the blue-collar working class or with their corporate desk jobs, all the while wreaking havoc on innocent souls when they clock out.

Though, Legion sees them for who they really are. Wolves in sheep's clothing. Beasts in human skin.

Cage is quiet as I trim the judge's wispy, thin hair, then remove his dentures and the few remaining teeth and start up the Sawzall again, dismembering him quickly. Except the second I finish silencing the machine, his deep, oceanic voice is back.

"When did you start working for Legion?"

I take a steady breath, grabbing two severed arms and walking them over to the first pen with Dill and Chili inside. I toss an annoyed glance toward Cage on the way, but his expectant expression doesn't budge.

"Not long after I came back. I bought this farm on a whim. It was cheap, secluded, and came with the pigs. I was going to get rid of them, but then I realized they could be useful. *I* could be useful."

The arms go flying into the pen, and Dill and Chili don't hesitate to tear into them. Pivoting, I head back toward the table and grab two legs. I heave them up, and when Cage steps toward me as if to help me, I shoot him a warning glare.

I've never needed a man to do the heavy lifting for me before, and I sure as fuck don't now. I'm more than capable.

Garlic and Paprika are fed next, and Cage doesn't remove his burning stare from me for a single second.

It sets me aflame, like a fever ravaging my insides. I'm short of breath, my palms are sweaty, and my knees are weak. I'd love to pretend that it's because he makes me sick, but my tightened nipples and the faint thrum between my thighs speak otherwise. He holds my body beneath his thumb, ready to betray me when my head demands control.

"I still had Legion's contact info and reached out. Told him I wanted to help snuff every piece-of-shit pedophile from this planet, and how I planned to do it. He was happy to oblige." I end my explanation with a shrug, before grabbing the two severed heads.

Oregano always gets the heads. She's the momma of the bunch—and the biggest.

He's quiet again, seeming to contemplate that as he watches Oregano bite into the judge's head, cracking it open like a watermelon.

"When did you start working for him?" I ask quietly.

"I don't. I still own my store, *Black Portal*. However, Legion's a friend, so when he needs help, I give him a hand."

I nod, turning my gaze back to my pigs. They were already named when I inherited them, and when I first heard what they were, I thought they were stupid. Who names pigs after seasoning?

Now, I find them quite fitting, considering their diets. A little bit of spice with their human meat.

"Moll—"

"You're supposed to call me Marie," I say. "That's what everyone else knows me by."

I flick a glance at him, noting his raised brow.

"Everyone else?"

I shrug. "The grocery store clerk that sells me wine, mainly."

"No friends? Boyfriend?"

I sigh and grab the other set of arms and legs, tossing them to Oregano. The other four can split the two torsos.

"I don't allow attachments when I make money the way I do. Lying to loved ones and living a double life doesn't appeal to me."

"So, you have no one," he states.

After tossing the torsos in the last two pens, I give him a dead stare, letting him see through the windows of my soul, only to find nothing inside.

"No one," I echo, then turn and head to the cleaning station tucked into the far corner of the barn, near the metal table.

"Legion already paid for tonight. Thanks for dropping them off," I toss over my shoulder, signaling the end of his visit. The pigs are finishing up, and I prefer to clean alone.

Or maybe I just prefer to *be* alone.

It's a quiet existence, but it's been so long since I've known anything else.

"I'll see you around, Molly," Cage murmurs, the statement sounding more like a vow than a goodbye.

My throat tightens, and it doesn't ease until I hear his car door slam shut, the engine start, and the tires crunching over the gravel as he retreats.

My phone rings, showing an unknown number, and like every time before, I answer it and hold it to my ear wordlessly.

"Is it done?"

"Yep."

"Good."

The line goes dead, and once again, I'm left with nothing more than blunt teeth chewing through bone.

"Thanks, Helga," I sigh.

chapter five

MOLLY

PRESENT
2022

THE SUDDEN KNOCK ON the door causes me to jump out of my skin, nearly sending the wine in my glass splashing in my face and on the fantasy novel from Adeline Reilly that I'd been reading.

Heart thundering, I stare at my front door with widened eyes, my brain running over possible scenarios on who the fuck could be at my door.

Of course, it jumps to the worst conclusions first.

What if it's a cop telling me that they've somehow pinned my father's murder on me and I'm under arrest. Or that they have evidence of me kidnapping Layla. Shit, maybe it's a friend of Francesca's, and they've come to collect what they feel they're owed.

The second knock has me snapping out of my spiraling thoughts. I hurriedly set my wine down on the coffee table, before scrambling to my room to grab my Glock. I've never had to use it, but I don't mind breaking it in.

Whoever it is, I'll feed them to my pigs and no one will ever kn—

A third knock.

Quietly, I fish out my phone from my back pocket and click on the feed for my security cameras, finding Cage on the other side of my door.

I release a weighted breath and swing open the door, glaring at him with annoyance.

He raises a brow.

"Can't say I've ever gotten that look before when showing up at a lady's door. I must be losing my charm." Then, he clocks the gun in my hand, and the other brow joins the first. "That's *also* new. You gonna use that on me, little ghost? I don't mind joining you in the afterlife."

"You scared me half to death," I snap. "What are you doing here?"

It's been a week since his first drop-off, and I wasn't prepared to see him again until the next delivery, which hasn't been scheduled yet.

He raises his hand, and for the first time, I notice he's holding a bouquet of tiger lilies, already in a beautiful crystal vase.

"I come bearing gifts." He lifts his other hand and holds up a DVD. "And a movie."

I sputter, unprepared for both items. He takes advantage and slides past me, forgoing an invitation.

"What the fuck," I mutter beneath my breath, dumbfounded as he kicks off his shoes at the entrance, then saunters into my living room and sets the tiger lilies on the center of the coffee table.

Though, he does pause to take a peek around.

My house is warm and cozy and newly updated. It has a rustic barn feel, with brown wooden beams across the ceiling, distressed wooden floors and furniture, and deep green cabinetry that complements my sage green couch and cream rugs. It isn't a large home, but it's perfect for me.

"You're having wine?" Cage asks, noticing the open bottle and my glass on the table. "My mom loves that shit—she'd love you. Anyway, I brought *The Silence of the Lambs.* Have you seen it?"

"Uh, no."

He shoots me a bewildered look over his shoulder, which quickly morphs into a devilish grin.

"I think you'll like it. It's a fucking cult classic. I figured you'd find some enjoyment out of it, considering it's about eating people."

I frown. "You think just because I feed my pigs humans, I'm into cannibalism?"

He shrugs, popping the disc into my DVD player to get the film ready. "I'm into whatever you're into. I get the feeling these types of movies are right up your alley. Come sit. I'll make popcorn."

I don't sit.

In fact, I stare at him as he walks over to my kitchen and starts rifling through the cabinets like he owns the place, finding a large bowl and my popcorn.

"What if I didn't have popcorn?" I question, crossing my arms.

Again, he peers at me from over his shoulder. His beauty is wicked, and I hate the way it makes my heart flutter.

"Everyone has popcorn, Molly." He says that like it's obvious.

And I suppose it is, considering it's been a staple in my household for the last several years.

He moves through the kitchen with confidence. Like he's been here all along and is as familiar with my home as he is with my body.

As much as my brain protests, my heart is softening.

I only knew him for a night, but I've missed him. More than I ever realized.

Sighing, I relent and trudge over to the couch. Instantly, I grab the wineglass, chugging the rest of it and hoping it calms the butterflies flapping around in my stomach.

"Don't worry, baby, I'll get more wine, too," he drawls, amusement in his tone.

I roll my eyes, but secretly, I like that he's here. Even though I wasn't prepared for an impromptu movie night, the idea of it actually sounds really fucking nice.

I don't think I've ever had one before. At least not one where I wasn't alone.

In no time, the delicious aroma of buttery popcorn fills the house, and he's sitting next to me on the couch with the snack, an uncracked bottle of wine, and an extra glass for himself.

I pop a piece of popcorn in my mouth and cast a thin-eyed look his way. "You could've called, ya know."

"I don't have your number, though."

I raise a brow. "Are you saying you're not a resourceful man?"

He shoots me a cocky grin. "I didn't want to give you the chance to say no."

He grabs the remote and presses play before I can formulate a proper response. We both know he's right, and in a weird way, I'm glad he took the option out of my hands.

I would've agonized over the proposal for far too long, talked myself out of doing it, and then regretted it later.

As the disturbing movie plays, we power through the popcorn like we're starving and drink the entire bottle of wine. And like a true gentleman, he lets me eat all the half-popped kernels.

Then, he grabs my legs and, resting them over his lap, massages my feet, all the while quoting lines from the film. The act is so thoughtless, so genuine, that tears rush to my eyes.

Never have I had anyone bring me flowers, set up a movie, and rub my feet. It's not something I even imagined for myself.

"Why did you come?" I ask softly after about an hour into the movie. My head is swimming a little, but I gaze at him with perfect clarity.

He glances at me. "I wanted to spend time with you. I missed you."

It's a simple answer, yet my heart is climbing into my throat.

"Thank you," I whisper.

He leans down and places a soft kiss on the top of my foot, then turns his focus back to the movie.

I haven't been to Cage's store, *Black Portal*, since that day nine years ago, desperate for an escape and hoping to God I'd find one in Cage.

He provided it for me, but it wasn't the escape I thought I needed.

Now that I'm here again, watching him sell a TV to a typical customer, I realize I'm finding one in him now.

It's been a few days since our movie night, and I don't think I've ever texted anyone so much in my life.

He asked for my number after our movie night, promising he'd call before showing up. Reluctantly, I gave it to him, but I hadn't expected him to text me so often. At first, I was hesitant to respond, but his charm was as addicting through the phone as it was in person, and ultimately, I found myself replying to him until it became thoughtless.

It's been superficial—neither of us daring to tread too deeply. I know he's overflowing with questions. Since I came in today, he's been staring at me with a burning curiosity when he thinks I'm not paying attention yet. But I haven't found the voice to tell him anything.

Admittedly, I'm too scared to.

I'm ashamed of my past. Ashamed of giving Layla up. And ashamed that I came running back when I couldn't find happiness thousands of miles away from her.

And maybe a little ashamed that I didn't have the gall to reconnect with him sooner—the only man who made me feel something outside of bone-crushing terror.

I'm sitting behind the counter, watching him work. He invited me to keep him company until the end of his shift. Even though he's the owner, he tries to stick to a schedule alongside his employees, considering it's his skills that are required to provide his real services.

"You are just so smart. I've no idea how to work these damn things anymore, but my grandson's been asking me to get one of these flat-screen TVs for his video games. And, well, I'll do anything for that kid," the older woman explains, waving her wrinkled hand around as she speaks.

Cage grins, which is a complete cause for concern. Every time he does, I swear that poor woman's heart stops, and an uncontrollable smile overtakes her wrinkled face.

"Well, then, who am I to get in the way of that? I'll point you in the direction of the most cost-efficient TV that'll make his heart happy. Sounds good, yeah?"

The woman titters. "So kind of you. Thank you, young man."

They walk off, leaving me alone with Silas, Cage's employee. We both glance at each other and then simultaneously roll our eyes.

"It's annoying how he's only gotten more charming with age," Silas grumbles, flicking his black hair from his equally dark eyes.

He's a handsome man himself, but his eyes tend to stray toward people who look a lot more like Cage.

"Whatever pays the bills, I guess," I respond, though Silas is right. He's only become more enigmatic since I've last seen him.

Which is definitely annoying.

"He never got over you, ya know," Silas says, bringing my attention snapping back to him. When my brows crease in confusion, he explains, "It took about three years and a really drunken night to admit that you both slept together that night." His arms rise defensively. "Which I'm not judging either of you for. Anyway, he blabbered on about how he hasn't been able to think of anyone else since. How every day, he would picture you showing back up in the store. I guess, in a way, he's been looking for you since you left, even if it was him that made you disappear."

My heart clenches painfully. It's a feeling that I understand.

Many nights, I questioned if I did the right thing by moving to Alaska. I would fantasize about what would happen if I went back and explored a different life—one with Cage.

If it would be as good as I thought it could be. But I talked myself out of it every time, convinced that changing the course of my life over one night with a man was entirely stupid and presumptuous.

I'd never been in a relationship beforehand, and certainly not after, so what the fuck would I know about what's normal to feel after a one-night stand?

"He barely knew me," I finally muster, clinging to the only excuse I have for the two of us always being drawn to each other the way we have. It was just one night. People don't fall in love that quickly, and it would be insane to think otherwise.

"At one point in our lives, we don't know our soulmates at all. But that doesn't make them any less of one. Sometimes... sometimes you just know."

I frown, contemplating that.

Cage reappears before I can wrap my head around that, and he slaps his hands on the counter to draw our attention.

"I have a few things to finish up for a client, and then I'm set to go," he announces. Then, he tips his chin toward the back door. "Come back with me?"

Smiling tightly, I wave at Silas before following him through the back door.

My stomach flutters with nerves, and every time I look at Cage, I increasingly realize that maybe he's more than just a man I slept with once.

And that is utterly terrifying.

For the next hour, I watch him work. He's designing a new driver's license for a client who will now reside in Maine. *Black Portal* is just a front, but his real job is making people disappear and reappear with an entirely new identity. New name, social security card, birth certificate, and state of residence.

Just like he did for me.

It's fascinating to see what he does to legitimize their new life and make it seem as real as any other person.

"Why is this client disappearing?" I ask finally, when he's almost finished.

He flicks his eyes toward me. "He killed his daughter's rapist and murderer. He's out on bail, but his lawyer is confident he'll still serve about twenty-five to life for his crime."

I chew on my lip. "You're saving his life."

Cage shrugs. "I'm just ensuring he has one. That's all."

He shuts his computer down, then turns to me on the chair.

"Let's go grab some food, yeah? I know a great pizza place. They brew the best beer I've ever had."

I wrinkle my nose. "I'm allergic to beer."

His eyes round, and he looks almost devastated, which draws a smile to my lips.

"I'm so fucking sorry for you. They offer a few different cocktails."

I shrug. "I'm just here for the pizza. You can thank yourself for that fixation."

He grins, his eyes sparkling. "I'd like to think I'm responsible for a few fixations, but sure, we'll start with pizza."

My cheeks burn, his implication obvious. He's implying his cock would be another, and fuck him for being right.

His wicked grin widens. "Come on, little ghost. Let's go stuff that pretty little mouth."

Said mouth drops, and he grabs my hand, pulling me after him as he laughs.

What a dick.

He's lucky it's a really fucking nice one.

chapter six

MOLLY

FOURTEEN YEARS AGO
2008

Sweat soaks through my clothing, my curls matted to the back of my neck, as I stumble over another fallen branch. I gasp, scarcely catching myself on a nearby tree.

The sun rose, set, and rose for a second time. Over twenty-four hours have passed since I ran from Francesca's house. Too many hours to be subjected to the heat in the middle of June, though at least the shade from the trees offered some protection from direct sunlight.

I don't need a mirror to know that my face is sunburnt and tomato red. However, I've made it this far, I can go just a little longer.

Anything for Layla.

I'll risk everything for her, as long as I'm with her.

In the distance, there's a break in between the trees where a structure peeks through. My overworked heart stops in my chest, and for several moments, I can't breathe. Can't even blink. I'm terrified that if I do, it'll disappear, only a figment of my imagination.

If it's only an illusion—something my brain created to protect me from my harsh reality—I think I'll let myself burn to death, only so when I do crumble to ash, there'll be nothing left to put back together.

That same fear drives me forward, my feet tripping over the ground once more, though not from trees that have shed their bark, but from pure desperation.

My vision blurs with tears, and my nose burns from my effort to keep them at bay. I can't lose it now. Not when I'm so close to being able to find Layla again.

The graveyard of crooked branches and green leaves gives way to a blue, sunny sky, showcasing a quiet suburb of homes beneath.

My lips part, and a choked gasp leaks past the chapped skin. Once again, I'm running, this time toward the closest house. It's quaint and tan with freshly painted brown shutters. The type of home that burrows a happy, white-picket-fence type of family in its warm embrace.

In the front yard is a man mowing his lawn, muttering soundlessly beneath the loud buzz of the machine. He appears in his forties, with dark brown skin and a thick salt-and-pepper beard. Sweat glistens on his bald head and coats his t-shirt as he cuts the grass beneath the hot sun.

"Help!" I shout, though the single syllable shatters as it's forced through a throat lined with sharp gravel.

His head snaps up, revealing a startled gaze, his eyes widening further when he sees me barreling toward him.

"Help!" I repeat. "I was kidnapped, I need help!"

He quickly switches the mower off, the sudden silence amplifying my desperate cries. I nearly slip, the worn soles of my shoes no longer gaining any traction on the loose grass like they did on the forest floor.

He holds up his hands—to stop or catch me, I'm not sure—but I throw myself into them anyway. He grabs ahold of my biceps, and though he's taken aback, his grip is firm.

A sob bursts from my throat, and another choked plea for help follows suit.

"Please, help me. Please, please!"

"Hey, hey, it's okay, you're safe. Let's... shit, Latoya!" He trips over his words, ending it with a desperate call for who I assume is his wife.

"You're safe now, it's okay— Latoya! Latoya, get out here!"

A door creaks and a soft voice asks, "What's going on? Who is that?" Urgency taints the last few notes of her second question, and I hear the rapid trek of her footsteps coming toward me.

"She—she just came running out of the woods calling for help," he explains, his words jumbling together.

"I was kidnapped," I squeak through another sob, my face planted firmly in the man's chest. He smells of pine and leather, and it's such a nice change from body odor and cigarettes that it only makes me burrow deeper into his embrace.

"Oh my God, honey, let's get her inside. She looks dehydrated!" Soft, warm skin envelops my hand, stirring the shot nerves to life. "Hey, sweetie, you're okay. Come inside," she urges gently.

I let her pull me away from her husband, only to be greeted with the warmest, chocolate brown eyes I've ever seen. Short, silky black curls billow around her deep brown skin, and she stares at me like a mother concerned for a child.

"Oh, you're sunburnt, too! Come on, sweetheart, let's get you cooled down." Her gaze lifts above my head. "Baby, call the police. I'm sure she has a family who's worried sick."

I don't have the heart to tell her that the only family I have is too young to understand my disappearance.

The oxygen stutters from my lungs as she leads me inside, the cold air radiating from within almost a shock to my system. My teeth chatter as I'm led directly into a cute living room, though I feel nothing except relief.

"Sit here while we wait, honey. I'll get you some aloe and fresh lemonade," Latoya instructs gently.

Woodenly, I plop onto a plush taupe couch. It complements the tan walls and pink and brown floral accents placed around the area. A soft yellow glow emits from a tall lamp tucked in the corner to my right, which stands next to a mahogany fireplace, a flat-screen TV mounted above.

Latoya returns a minute later with a bottle of aloe. Gently, she applies some to my cheeks and nose. The motherly affection radiating from her has tears pricking the backs of my eyes.

"There you go," she whispers affectionately. "Now sit tight, I'll be right back."

She scurries off toward where I assume the kitchen is, while her husband comes through the front door. He pauses when he sees me, and his brown eyes soften.

"You look worn out, my dear," he comments. "Police are on their way. Do you need anything while we wait?"

I shake my head, feeling terrible for bursting into their lives in such a horrible way, yet so relieved that they let me.

"What's your name, sweetheart?" he asks, sitting on the matching couch across from me.

"Molly."

"That's a pretty name, Molly. You can call me Devin. How old are you?"

"Twenty."

My answers are robotic, and now that I'm... *safe*, I can't feel anything at all. None of this feels real. It's an out-of-body experience, and though I can hear and see everything around me, I'm unable to process any of it.

My heart rate picks up as Devin continues to pepper me with questions. Blackness leaks into the edges of my vision, and I begin to wonder if this is a good idea.

What if Rocco shows up, and hurts Devin and Latoya? Would that make me responsible for their deaths?

Images of Latoya and Devin lying in pools of blood flash through my head, their eyes open and lifeless. Senseless deaths. And it's all my fault.

I shouldn't be here.

I'm going to get them killed.

My knees crack from how quickly I stand. "I-I have to go," I stammer, feeling my pulse thrumming wildly in my throat.

Devin slowly rises to his feet, lifting his hands in a placating gesture.

"Hey, hey, you're safe now, Molly."

I may be safe with them, but they are not safe with *me*.

"I just can't be here. They're going to be looking for me, and I don't want you and your wife to get hurt."

A crease forms between his brows. "The poli—"

I dart for the door, nearly crashing into Latoya, who's carrying a glass full of lemonade. She gasps and stumbles out of the way, ice and liquid sloshing over the rim and onto her hand.

"I'm sorry! I have to go before they find me. Th-thank you for your help!"

Latoya opens her mouth, but I'm flinging open the front door and flying out of the house before she can manage a sound.

My head is swiveling left and right, finding the street empty, yet convinced that Rocco and his men are here, lurking just out of sight and waiting for the right moment to strike.

Adrenaline is flooding my system, sending dangerous levels of toxins into my bloodstream. I don't feel the heat any longer, only utter panic that I'm going to be running right back into my captors' hands.

I bolt off the front porch, Latoya's concerned voice calling after me as I take off down the street.

There has to be a bus station around here somewhere, right? I've no idea where we are—didn't even think to ask. But it doesn't appear I'm still in Montana with how different the mountains look.

I run down the street, keeping to the backyards of the houses so I'm out of view. Within a minute, there's a police car turning a corner, likely heading to Latoya and Devin's house.

Ducking behind a playground set, I wait for it to pass before darting away again. After running through a few more yards, I spot a little kid playing outside ahead, his parents out of sight. He appears to be around nine or ten years old, wearing swim shorts and a tank top, kicking around a soccer ball. His pale skin is flushed from the heat, turning the entirety of his cheeks and nose bright red.

He stares at me blankly as I slink up to him, keeping light on my feet as if Rocco will be able to hear me from wherever he is.

"Hey, kid. What state is this?" I whisper, glancing toward his house, where a sliding glass door is directly in view.

"Oregon," he answers casually, curiosity piqued in his crystal blue eyes.

I bite my lip, not liking how far from home I am. Guess it could be much worse.

"Do you know where a bus station is?"

He shakes his head. "I can ask my dad."

"No!" I whisper-shout just as he takes a step toward his house. He pauses, a little startled but still curious.

"Sorry. Uh, would you know where downtown is?" I ask, my paranoia growing stronger with each passing second.

What if Rocco finds me with this kid? They'd probably take him, too, and it'd be all my fault.

I *need* to get out of here.

He tips his chin up as he thinks, showcasing gaps and two different-sized front teeth. His lips are bright red, as if he chugged cherry juice.

Hurry the fuck up. Your life is on the line!

"I think you go that way—" He whips his arm out behind him, pointing straight ahead of me. "—and then you will see a McDonald's, and I think that's downtown."

He ends his shitty directions with a shrug, peering back at me with a *was that good?* expression.

I tighten my lips into a firm line. I'm not much better off, but at least I know I'm going in the right direction.

"Thanks, kid." I pat his head, then take off again. "Oh, and don't talk to strangers!" I call out behind me.

"But you're a stranger," he counters loudly.

And I easily could've gotten you killed.

I don't say that, too far away to tell him about the horrors of this evil world. The only thing I can do is hope his parents protect him from it, unlike my own.

Because, mine... mine are the ones who sold me to Francesca.

And I'll be damned if I allow them to do the same with Layla.

chapter seven

CAGE

PRESENT
2022

My left foot taps against the footrest as I drive down the lengthy gravel road leading toward Molly's house. Or, I guess *Marie's* house, though I'll never be able to call her that. Molly was the name I groaned over and over when I was inside her nine long years ago. And it's the name that still comes back to haunt me during my loneliest hours.

"You could've warned me," I growl through the phone. I've been calling the fucker since the first delivery to Molly's house, and coincidentally, he's been busy.

"That was my error," Legion says, his voice just as deep and toneless as it always is. "I hadn't realized you formed an attachment to her."

Dickhead. That was definitely a dig.

"Then why didn't you tell her I was coming? She seemed surprised."

"I should have," he concedes. "I let her know a good friend of mine was coming in lieu of Eli until he recovers, and that you were trustworthy. She trusts me so she didn't seem concerned with your name."

I sigh. "Why didn't you tell me she came back?"

I'm pissed that he didn't. Not because she reversed everything I did to keep her hidden and safe. No, it's because she's been back, within reach, and I never fucking knew. She doesn't owe me shit. Except there's a small part of my ego that hoped she'd want to see me again. The fact that she didn't, only makes me want to prove just how fucking wrong she is for feeling that way. And the problem is I don't know if she'll let me have her, but I do know it won't stop me.

None of this has anything to do with Legion. Not really. He may employ her, but who she was before isn't of much concern to him. The only thing he does make his business is who his employees are now.

"I didn't know I was required to," he counters dryly.

I growl beneath my breath. "Why did she?"

He sighs. "If I recall, she has a sister who was given up for adoption before she left. I assume her reasons for returning to Montana may have something to do with that," Legion says.

I exhale slowly. I only had one night with her. And admittedly, we didn't do too much talking. Although I did know from the news reports after she went missing that she had a much younger sister. Layla, I think her name was.

So, if Molly's willing to return to the one place that caused her so much distress, then it can only be for someone as important as Layla.

"Do you know where her sister is now?"

"Yes," he answers shortly.

I wait, but he doesn't elaborate.

"Legion," I growl, my patience waning.

"Do I need to be concerned about what you will do with said knowledge?"

"No."

He's silent for a beat, but I know I've won when I hear his exasperated exhale.

"She's fifteen years old now, and lives with a nice, wealthy family. And that is not to be messed with, Cage."

I'd happily fucking kidnap her if that's what Molly asked, but I keep that to myself. Obviously, Legion would find that concerning.

"We're clear," I clip. "Thanks, man. I'll report when the delivery is complete."

I toss my phone to the passenger seat, releasing another heavy exhale. There's an undeniable burning desire to know everything about Molly. Why was Layla given up for adoption? And did Molly return, because she wants her sister back? Or to be around for when she turns eighteen?

The obsession is familiar.

It's similar to what I felt when she was first kidnapped. The intrigue of her disappearance and what happened to her—I was incredibly transfixed by her case.

The girl who not only vanished out of thin air but seemed to lose her mind beforehand.

The footage showed her walking into the gas station, and five minutes later, she was running from something that the security cameras couldn't see. Throwing things on the floor, clearly in distress, while absolutely destroying the place. And then seeming to calm, as if someone had forced her to.

What was more disturbing was that the cameras didn't see her leave the gas station. Same with the ones outside the back exit—that door never opened, and she was never seen walking out.

At 9:02 PM, she waved goodbye to the man behind the counter, walked out of shot toward the back door, and that was the last the world saw of Molly.

It was riveting, and I was fascinated.

But this obsession that I feel now is still not the same. No—it's *exactly* what I felt when I met her. *Had* her.

The girl with haunted eyes and a perpetual frown, who carried a sadness so deep that it permanently altered the shape of her lips.

I spent the night tracing my tongue along her Cupid's bow until I remolded her mouth to fit against mine. Because as long as I was inside her, her sadness would be powerless to my obsession. And there would be no part of her that wasn't made precisely for me.

I pull up to her farm, seeing the glow emanating from the same lone window in her house. It's been a week since I last saw her, and I've been talking myself down from showing up at her house uninvited again.

I wonder if that light is shining from her bedroom. Now, I can't look away without first imagining the silhouette of her naked body shadowed behind the glass. The curve of her pert breasts, just big enough to fill my hands, and those dusty pink nipples I could barely pull my mouth away from that night. The swell of her plump ass, before curving into those creamy thighs.

Fuck.

My cock is straining painfully against my zipper, and I'm tempted to unzip and stroke myself to the fantasy. It's not nearly as graphic as it could be, but part of me doesn't want to guess what her matured body looks like now. Mainly because I've already convinced myself I'll find out soon enough, and I want to take her in without any preconceived notions.

It may be the only good thing about not seeing her for almost a decade. I'll get to experience her for the first time all over again.

Reaching into my pocket, I pull out my pack of nicotine gum and pop one in my mouth, needing the buzz to relax my nerves. Then, I get out of the car just as she emerges from the depths of the barn.

She gazes at me cautiously, her stare sliding down my form, then back up again.

"How many?"

"Just one tonight."

Without a word, she twists on her heel and disappears inside the barn.

My heart is pounding, and I'm not even sure why anymore. Anticipation has gathered between the crevices of my bones, as if I'm gearing up to commit the worst of my crimes.

Maybe I am. Yet, I can't find it in me to give a fuck.

Just like last time, I drag the corpse out of my trunk and carry the dead woman into Molly's barn. She's dressing in her protective suit while I drop the body on the metal table.

The silence is heavy and filled with electrical currents. If I licked my thumb and held it up, I'd wield lightning in a matter of seconds. The ways I'd use that to my advantage...

The loud buzz of the hair clippers rips my thoughts straight out of the gutter and into the hands of the woman cutting off another person's hair, preparing to dismember her. She already undressed the woman, and I hadn't even realized it.

I watch her, riveted, and remembering the twenty-five-year-old girl who walked into my TV store, asking for help with her shoulders curled inward and her eyes watching over her shoulder with every step. To this moment, a woman who is so calm and standing like she's sure of herself. It's such a contrast to the version of her I once knew that I'm nearly frothing at the mouth to get to know who she is now.

She finishes shaving the woman's head, then extracts her teeth quickly and meticulously—so smoothly that it only shows her experience.

And when she begins to saw through the corpse's head, I can't help but feel my fascination with her deepening.

Unsurprisingly, I find her skillset in dismembering a person attractive.

"What did she do?" she asks after finishing removing the head.

"She sold her kid to her boyfriend. He would pay for his drug habit with her daughter's body."

She pauses, the vibrating blade an inch away from the woman's leg. She clutches the tool until her rubber gloves squeak from the force of her grip, and when she continues to stay frozen, my brows plunge, concern trickling in.

"Molly."

She jumps, just the slightest, then hurries to continue removing the woman's leg at the hip.

"Where's the boyfriend?" she questions, her tone stiff.

"With Legion. I'm sure I'll be delivering his body soon."

She nods, moving to the second leg.

"And the girl?"

"Probably at a Z location."

Her head turns just enough to give me a hint of her high cheekbones and plump lips. Redness mottles her pale flesh, darkening the light dusting of freckles on her cheeks.

"Find out for me?" she asks quietly.

Something about the young girl's situation has struck a nerve with Molly, which only further ignites the burning curiosity to know more about her past.

"I can do that," I promise, satisfying her enough to where she resumes her bloody task.

The pigs behind me are creating a ruckus, the scent of blood getting them excited.

"Is there a reason why you want me to look into her?" I question, desperate for even a crumb.

She doesn't respond. Not until she's finished completely removing the limbs from the woman's torso.

"Doesn't matter. I'd just like to know she's safe."

She's evading my question—keeping me in the dark—which only stirs the demon lurking inside my soul. A beast who doesn't like to be kept in a darkness it can't manipulate.

I already feel the blackness unleashing into my system, and my fingers crack with how hard I clench them.

The thought of anyone hurting her, especially if it was in the same way that little girl was hurt, will easily turn me into a bloodthirsty monster. The worst part is that I *know* she was hurt. I know whoever kidnapped her didn't bring her to a place that respected her body.

She may have already disposed of them. But if not, I'd love nothing more than to kill them myself.

"Molly," I warn, my tone deepening with anger.

She freezes, much like she did when I first shared the woman's crimes against her kid.

"Did the same thing happen to you?" I ask boldly.

My obsession won't let her get out of not telling me every little fucking detail about her life. About her past and all the reasons she ran to Alaska, and the reasons she decided to come back and make a living out of feeding pedophiles to her pigs.

I've held off long enough and refuse to hold back the burning questions any longer.

"It doesn't matter, Cage," she bites out, tearing the protective glasses off her face and tossing them on the table. The white teeth marks beneath her eye are brightened from the redness of her skin.

A testament to the horrors she survived.

She won't look at me as she picks up the severed head and stomps over to the pen with one monstrous pig inside and nearly launches it in.

The pig wastes no time cracking open the skull. I'm standing right beside its pen, so I shift a few feet away to avoid the spray of blood while Molly angrily marches back toward the table. I watch her silently as she repeats the process with the torso and both legs.

I've lost my patience by the time she snatches one of the arms from the nearly empty table, then stomps back toward me, preparing to throw it in one of the pens. I grab onto her bicep before she does. Whether it's instinct or because she likes to beat people with spare limbs when she's pissed, her arm whips out, and the bloody arm comes careening toward my head.

I duck out of the way, though I'm not spared from blood spattering across my face. I grab onto her wrist, meeting her searing glare.

"Did I say something to piss you off, my little ghost?" I ask wickedly.

She snarls and tugs on her arm, failing to tear it out of my grip.

She looks like she wants to run again, peering at me like an animal backed into a corner. Her flight mode is activated, and I have no fucking qualms with hunting her down.

"You have no right!" she shouts, panting heavily as she seethes at me. "You don't get to come back into my life and start demanding things from me. The only thing you get to do is bring me pig food, and then you *leave*."

The fire in her green eyes is captivating. Fuck, I'm so enthralled.

"You're breathtaking," I murmur.

She blinks at me, taken aback and speechless for several moments.

"W-what? Why would you say that?"

Because staring into her eyes is the only thing I needed, to convince myself she's everything I'll ever want for as long as oxygen invades my lungs. I knew it deep in my bones the day I met her. Even back then, my soul immediately recognized hers as its other half.

"Because I'd tell you anything," I answer. "There's not a single thing I'd be able to keep from you. Especially when you look so goddamn beautiful."

Her hand slackens, shock colored on every inch of her ethereal face.

I take advantage and slide the severed arm out of her hold. Then, I toss it across the barn and into one of the pigpens.

She glances to the side, seemingly trying to gather herself.

"You're going to find every drop of blood that went past the plastic and clean it up. This is an active crime scene that can never look like one when they're done eating."

I grin, and her stare latches onto my mouth, her own lips parting subconsciously.

"That must mean I'm not allowed to leave yet," I drawl lazily.

She wrinkles her nose in distaste at my comment, then attempts to extract her wrist from my grip again. I don't release her—*won't* release her. Holding her is too addictive, and I haven't had nearly enough.

"Let me go, Cage," she demands breathlessly, tugging her arm more insistently.

"I've already done that once," I say, tugging her into my chest roughly. Her gasp feathers across my chest, setting the muscle inside aflame. I lower my mouth to her ear, evoking a shiver that overtakes the entirety of her body. "I'm not doing it again."

"Cage," she squeaks out, even as my lips are already tracing the soft outer shell of her ear, where a dainty gold ring is pierced. Her skin is spotless from blood here, and I intend to take advantage of that. I flick my tongue against the metal, and another helpless sound emits from her throat.

And that's what makes her so goddamn exciting. She's *not* helpless, but I sure as fuck like it when she plays the part.

"We can't do this," she insists, her words airy and lacking conviction.

"Not this, either?" I query before catching the piercing between my teeth and sucking it gently.

Her other hand flies to my chest, her bloody glove covering my shirt in crimson.

I retreat just far enough to whisper, "Now we're going to need to burn that."

She swallows thickly, the sound audible yet quiet.

It seems to take her a second to gather herself, and then she's croaking, "Then take it off."

I assess her closely to ensure she's not fucking with me, but she keeps her gaze locked onto the bloody handprint over my heart. She could be lying, planning to bolt the second I release her.

Deciding that I wouldn't mind the chase, I unlock my fingers from her wrist, one digit at a time.

Her chest heaves, and my cock strains against my zipper, imagining how hard her nipples must be beneath her suit. I intend to find out.

Watching her closely, I slowly remove my leather jacket, having enough foresight to throw it away from the blood. Then, I grab the back of my collar and pull the soft fabric over my head.

Immediately, her burning stare falls to my bare chest, then onto my stomach, tracing every muscle I've worked my ass off for. The industry I work in doesn't allow for weak muscles and little strength. Criminals are my clients, and, at any moment, I may have to defend myself. There have been plenty of times when I *have* had to.

Her tongue darts out, wetting her bottom lip as she dissects every inch of my exposed flesh.

"I don't..." She licks her lips again, this time nervously. "I don't remember you having that many muscles before."

I quirk a brow. "Baby, I was twenty-seven the last time you saw me shirtless. A lot has changed since then."

"Right," she mumbles, once more distracted by the view.

I close the space between us, biting my lip to contain my devilish smile as her breath stutters from her throat.

"I want you to show me what has changed with you, but I also want to see what's the same." Her next swallow is audible. "Does that spot between your tits still get red when you come?"

I crowd into her, instigating by bumping my chest against hers and inhaling her sweet vanilla and cinnamon scent. It mingles with the unmistakable smell of copper, which only serves to make her more enticing.

Molly is painted in blood, and I want her to cover me in it, too.

She stumbles, a small whimper reaching my ears. It isn't born of fear or weakness but of a woman overcome with her emotions.

Before she can overthink all the reasons this is a bad idea, I grab the zipper at the hollow of her neck and pull down, the teeth breaking apart the only backdrop to her uneven breathing.

The material parts to reveal heaving breasts covered by a thin, white tank top. She shrugs out of it, the oversized gloves effortlessly falling off with the yellow suit. Then, it falls down her legs completely, revealing tiny black shorts and toned, long legs.

She's tall, at least five-ten, and has the most delicious curves. She's fucking perfect for me. Every little facet of her was designed just for me.

Chewing on her bottom lip, she steps out of the suit, along with her black rubber boots, and kicks them to the side.

Barefoot and defenseless, yet she stands like a trained killer, and I know her most valuable weapons are her hands.

She's fucking *beautiful.*

A loud bang from the pens disturbs the tense silence, causing Molly to startle. The pigs are demanding to be fed again.

"We're all hungry, baby. Who are you going to feed first?" I ask wickedly before gliding my tongue across my bottom lip.

I'm fucking *starving.*

She doesn't remove her challenging gaze as she deliberately steps away and toward the metal table. I can sense how predatory my own stare is, but the red flush crawling up to her cheeks indicates she doesn't mind being my prey.

She grabs the last remaining body part from the table—another arm. Then, she walks it over to one of the pens where two pigs eagerly await the last of their meal. The others are still working their way through the torso and legs.

Maintaining eye contact, she holds out the arm and drops it in, blood spraying across the hay as they tear it apart.

I stride toward her, my own blood heating as she worries her bottom lip and her hands begin to fidget.

"You know, your pets would tear you apart in seconds with all that nervous energy," I comment, amusement coloring my tone.

She narrows her eyes. "Then it's so fortunate for me that I know how to defend myself."

I grin, the act as devilish as my intentions.

I round her, sliding my chest against her back as I lean down to whisper in her ear. "You must be frightening."

"I am," she insists, though her voice is breathless, and another tremor is working its way down her spine.

I hum, reaching up to tuck a stray curl behind her ear.

Again, she shivers.

"Then show me, my little ghost."

chapter eight

MOLLY

PRESENT
2022

I HAVE TUNNEL VISION.

There's only a sliver of light, the small orb blurring as I process his challenging words.

Then show me.

Show him years upon years of practice that I never utilized because I refused to put myself in a situation where I'd *have* to. Yet here I am.

A dangerous man at my back demanding to see what I'm made of. The honest answer is trauma, sadness, and scars that I can't bear to look at. But I still feel them.

Just as I do the predator breathing down my neck.

I wait a few moments, each second ticking in my pulse, and then I'm twisting at the waist and sending my elbow flying toward his mouth.

He jerks back, and I only manage to clip him, but that was only a distraction. Before he can prepare for anything else, my heel smashes into his foot, causing him to stumble. Then, I'm advancing on him, keeping light on my feet as I strategically strike him in succession, meant to both keep his attention on my hands and lull him into a pattern.

I send my fists flying toward his head, which he blocks, but my foot is already hooked around his ankle, and the next second, his legs are in the air as he slams flat on his back.

I'm straddling him before he can process it, and a grunt bursts from his mouth. But he recovers quickly, flipping me onto the plastic covering before I can blink.

A breath escapes me, and I kick up my legs until my tailbone is lifted, wrapping my legs around his head to keep him at arm's length.

I squeeze my thighs tightly, and he curls his lips into a salacious smile.

"Can't say I'm mad about this development," he rasps.

Before I can respond, he grabs my sides and squeezes, hitting a ticklish spot that causes me to jump and loosen my thighs. He makes quick work of slipping his head free and flipping me onto my stomach.

I manage to make it to my knees before he bars his arm across my throat and holds my back against his front tightly. His other hand sensually glides up my stomach, stopping short of my breasts.

Though it doesn't stop my pussy from tightening in anticipation, searching for something to fill it.

"You're wound so tight, baby. Need me to help loosen you up?" he instigates, his deep voice wicked and rough, sending a tsunami of chills down my spine.

Panting, I still, my brain circulating over the different moves I could make. His hard cock is pressed against my backside, showing me just how much he's enjoying the fight.

Snarling, I send the back of my head flying into his nose, eliciting another grunt. His arm relaxes just enough for me to slip out from beneath it, spin, and tackle his ass, straddling him for a second time.

A bead of crimson trails out of his nose, yet somehow, it only makes me more ravenous. Just like my pigs, the sight of his blood makes me feral.

His hands grip either side of my hips, and he pulls me down against him as he grinds his cock against my clit, sending a shock wave of pleasure shooting up my body.

A quiet moan leaves his throat, a sound that I'm instantly swallowing as I crash my lips against his.

I know the breath was knocked out of his lungs, and I don't intend to allow him to have it back.

A growl builds in his throat and reverberates beyond my teeth, followed by a sharp nip to my bottom lip. It only makes me kiss him harder, in which he returns with tenfold the passion. His hands are plunging into my curls, fisting them tightly, using his grip on them to anchor my head and move his lips over mine however he pleases. Before I know it, he's taken over completely, and I'm helpless to stop him.

I've worked hard to defend myself against a man's touch, but one kiss from Cage is fucking paralyzing.

Just like he swore, he acts as if he's starving, devouring me as he plunges his tongue into my mouth and curls it sinfully against mine.

I'm entirely lost to him as he tears at the white tank top, ripping the fabric in half and roughly pushing it off my body. My sports bra is next to fall victim to his fiery touch, pulling it over my head and flinging it into the unknown.

Instantly, his hands are cupping my breasts, gnashing his teeth against mine.

"Let me taste," he demands roughly, his voice sounding as if his soul has been possessed by the king of hell.

I crawl up his body just enough for him to wrap his hot mouth around a nipple, his tongue swirling around the tightened bud before his teeth bite into the soft flesh.

My back bows while my hand flies into the short strands atop his head, crying out as the sting worsens.

Just when it becomes too much, he releases me only to suck my abused nipple back into his mouth, easing the pain with long, thorough licks.

The sounds coming from my throat are raspy and broken with pleasure. If my body was a kingdom, he'd be waging a celestial war against me where I'd easily crumble beneath his forces. The gods within have grown tired, and it's a relief to succumb to an inferno the devil created just for me.

Cage retreats again, and just when he begins to dish out another command, blood splatters across my face, neck, and side, and across his chest.

A startled scream leaves my throat, and I look over to see Chili tearing into the thigh of the butchered woman.

Mouth open in shock, I turn back to Cage, only to find him peering up at me with an emotion I don't know how to name. But what I do know is that it's powerful, unrestrained, and unlike anything I've seen before.

"You're fucking incredible," he says, his tone hushed.

Instinctively, I peer down at myself, where trails of blood paint my breasts, the valley between them, and my stomach.

I should be horrified, yet when I lift my stare back to Cage, I feel anything but. My clit throbs and arousal gathers deep in my core. The urge to grind against his cock is overwhelming, but I refrain for now.

Something wet splatters onto my face, then trails down my cheek before a crimson bead drips off my jaw and lands on my breast, all of which Cage watches intently.

His hands cup my hips, and he squeezes tightly. Feeling invigorated, I brush a black-painted nail across my nipple, my mouth parting in wonder as his stare drops to my chest. His eyes darken like a forest fire within, blackening with a hunger as potent as the flames. I've never been so ready to walk into a wildfire.

Teasingly, I smear the crimson over the swell and down to my ribs, where a macabre bird with its wings wired onto its body is tattooed.

The black-and-gray artwork snags his attention for a moment, but inevitably, he refocuses on my finger once it reaches the waistband of my shorts.

"Stand up," he rasps, anticipation gleaming in his eyes. He doesn't seem inclined to stand with me. Instead, he props up on his elbows and reclines back on them. He stares up at me with a reverence that can only be captured by the human eye. Nothing—not even our own hands—could recreate that image and do it any justice.

I do as he says, though my knees tremble and threaten to crumble as tragically as if they were an ancient monument.

"Take it all off, baby. I need to see everything," he commands hoarsely.

My heart pounds in my chest as I hook my thumbs beneath the fabric of my shorts and panties and slide them down my thighs. I kick them to the side where the rest of my clothes lay.

Insecurity and forced confidence battle for dominance. From his position, I know he can see the scar on my hip—a perfect imprint of teeth from when Dad bit me years ago. Sadly, it isn't the only bite mark forever marring my flesh. They're also on my biceps, stomach, thighs, and of course, my face.

He left them everywhere, sinking his teeth so far into me that I passed out from the pain. Most of the bite marks eventually faded, except the ones now on full display, crimson smeared over them.

"Jesus Christ," Cage groans. "Sit on my fucking face, Molly."

My stomach twists as I step over him, butterflies unleashing within as I crouch over his face, keeping my feet flat on the floor.

Cage was the last man I slept with, and something about that is utterly embarrassing. I've gotten intimate with plenty of vibrators throughout the years, though I could never muster the courage to let another man touch me again.

Nerves eat me alive, but the wet, hot slide of Cage's tongue along my slit has me forgetting exactly what I was anxious about. And his unrestrained moan that follows has my stomach tightening.

My mouth falls open as bliss consumes me, beginning at my core and spreading out to the tips of my fingers and toes.

"Oh," I breathe, my eyes rolling into the back of my head as his tongue spears inside me, circling around my inner walls.

A growl builds in his chest and his arms circle around my thighs, anchoring me onto his face. My legs tremble violently, once more threatening to give out on me. They're fucking useless when it comes to him.

"Fuck, baby, you taste so good," he groans against me, the vibrations sending another wave of bliss throughout me.

"Cage," I moan just as his tongue flicks at my clit. The breath in my lungs gets lost somewhere on the way out, taking a wrong turn and depriving me of precious oxygen.

I need to breathe, but I need to come in Cage's mouth so much more.

Lips parted and brows pinched, I peer down at Cage to find his heated stare already locked on mine.

The butterflies in my stomach become volatile. They're unable to handle Cage eating me alive—whether it's because they're frightened that they'll be devoured next, or if it's because they know that by the time he's done, I'll be in ruins and there will be nothing left of me. No home for them to live.

He sucks my clit into his mouth, his teeth grazing the sensitive flesh and sending goosebumps scattering across my skin. Already, I feel an orgasm building low in the pit of my stomach, and while I want nothing more than to lose myself in it, I don't know that I'm ready for the aftermath.

"Don't stop," I choke out despite myself.

He sucks harder, showing me that stopping is the last thing on his mind. Then, he releases my thighs and flattens his palms on my stomach before gliding them up to my breasts and cupping them roughly, smearing the blood further across my flesh.

His fingers pluck my nipples, and once again, I feel his teeth graze my clit. The threat is imminent, as if to say that if I don't come soon, I will be punished.

It's a warning that I have no choice but to heed.

His tongue continues to work me, and after a few more seconds, I feel myself approaching the mouth of a volcano, where I'll peer inside, only to be blown to smithereens by the catastrophic eruption.

His tongue flicks, and I'm leaning over the fiery mouth. It flicks again, and I'm completely decimated.

Vaguely, I hear the scream erupting from my mouth as violently as the orgasm washing over me. I think I cry out Cage's name, but at this moment, the only thing I can be sure of is that I'll never be the same once I come down.

Bright bursts of color explode in my otherwise blackened vision, and the entirety of my body seizes against his face. My hips gyrate mindlessly, where his tongue is still flattened against me.

By the time I come down, it feels like I've traveled light years and back. Like I have an entirely new lifetime of experiences.

Panting heavily, I open my eyes, though my vision is still blurred and unreliable. Cage is slipping out from beneath me, and the heat of his body envelops me a moment later, his front pressing into my back. Despite the warm air blowing through the open barn doors, I shiver.

"I have bad news," he whispers darkly.

"What's that?" I croak.

His hot breath fans across the shell of my ear, and the effect is no worse than when a predator is watching you and there's nowhere to run.

"I'm still hungry." His voice is as deep as a mountain and as rough as the rock it's made of.

My bottom lip finds itself between my teeth, and I clamp down until I feel a sharp sting.

I have no fucking idea what to say to that. All I know is that he could take whatever he wants from me, and I would gladly give it to him.

His rough palms fan across either side of my hips, leaving tiny little embers in his wake.

"I need more," he rasps.

"You can have me," I whisper.

Dangerous words to say to a predator, but it's been so long since I've felt this alive.

In response, I hear the clink of his metal belt buckle, followed by the sound of it pulling free from the loops of his black jeans.

My muscles swell with anticipation. For a moment, I'm transported back to when I was twenty-five with the same domineering presence crowding over me. And while it was terrifying, it was equally fucking thrilling.

Soft leather brushes across my neck, barely giving me time to register it before it's looped through the buckle and being pulled tight. My eyes round, and the startled sound from my throat scarcely escapes before it's constricted, allowing me just enough air to stay conscious.

Then, the telltale sign of metal teeth breaking apart follows. What little breath I have comes out in short, excited bursts. Fabric shuffles, and I glance over my shoulder to see him kneeling behind me, completely naked.

"You shouldn't be real," I croak.

He was beautiful nine years ago, but now, he's otherworldly. Surely, a mirage I've constructed in my brain after too many years of isolation. His body is made up of muscles packed beneath tattooed flesh. Solid, but lean. A perfect combination that creates a masterpiece da Vinci fucking wishes he had invented.

He reaches forward and brushes his thumb gently over the teeth prints on my cheekbone.

"I have a feeling you shouldn't be alive. Yet here you are." His stare is affectionate, though it borders on obsession. "And I'm so fucking lucky that you are."

I don't know if I'd ever consider myself lucky, but at this moment, I think I feel the same.

Then, he's tugging on the belt around my neck and roughly hauling me back into his chest. I gasp, my brain slow to process as my body conforms to his demands without thought. The pressure of his palm against my lower back follows, encouraging it to bow until I'm curved into a perfect C, my ass and the crown of my head pressed against him. His other hand cups the underside of my jaw, keeping me firmly in place.

He stares down at me with a savage expression, his mouth poised above mine.

"I love how easily you bend for me."

"Just don't expect me to break," I counter breathlessly.

He hums, as if that's yet to be determined. "But that's my favorite part," he croons against my lips.

His cock teases my entrance, slipping through my pussy with ease.

"Are you on birth control?"

"Yes," I breathe. "Though you should've asked sooner in case I wasn't."

He chuckles wickedly. "I still wouldn't have cared."

Before I can muster a response, he's pushing inside me. My mouth drops open, and he's licking my bottom lip, the act nearly as erotic as him splitting me in half. I'm trembling in his hold, and when he's halfway in, he pauses.

"Can't take it?" he asks devilishly.

"N—"

He drives himself completely inside me, not bothering to wait for my answer.

A choked scream greets his savage smile, burning pain at being stretched so suddenly taking over for a moment. But then he begins to roll his hips, and I'm reminded why he was impossible to forget after one night.

"I forgot to mention, you don't have a choice." He places a sweet kiss on my lips, something that would be a direct contrast to his words had it not felt condescending.

"Asshole," I choke out, though the word is weak as he easily dominates my pussy. My attention is already hyper-fixating on the intense pleasure radiating from between my thighs.

"Careful with the words that fall out of your mouth, baby. I might get confused and claim that, too."

"You wouldn't," I growl.

He pauses again, and his expression portrays utter conviction.

"I would do anything to show you that you're mine."

Somewhere between the beginning of his statement and the end, my heart worked its way inside my throat. I'm unable to speak or swallow, only stare at him in shock, for which he takes as confirmation to keep going as if he didn't just rock me to my core.

I blink, and he's fucking me again, tightening the belt around my throat until black spots swarm my vision, though careful not to cut off my oxygen completely.

This time, he sets a steady yet thorough pace, ensuring to watch my reactions closely. Within half a minute, he's targeted a sensitive spot inside me and focuses on stroking right there until my eyes are fluttering.

It shouldn't be so easy for someone to be able to pick me apart like that, but there's not a single inch of me that gives a fuck right now. I wouldn't even be capable if I tried.

"Cage," I moan, my brows furrowing as the sensations become too intense. I strain against his hold, attempting to curl my hips forward, if only so it gives me a moment to fucking breathe.

"Where're you going?" he barks, bringing me back to him. Then, he laughs, the sound savage. "Did you really think I couldn't break you when you can barely take me?" he questions arrogantly.

"I'm taking you just fine," I bite out, my eyes threatening to cross when he hits a spot that feels otherworldly.

"Then why are you trying to run away?" he whispers wickedly.

I want to slap him, but I'm so overwhelmed by the pleasure that I can hardly formulate a snappy response.

"Fuck," I cry, squeezing my eyes shut as he fucks me harder.

"I know you can do better, baby. Let me see you take my cock like a good little slut."

A sharp moan pours from my throat, followed by his name.

Once more, he's licking along the seam of my lips, as if to taste his name on my tongue. Just as his mouth covers mine, I feel a warm liquid splatter against my chest.

I flinch, my brain beginning to split and latch on to the fact that I'm being covered in more blood. The corner of his mouth tics up, and he releases my jaw—though his hold on the belt keeps me in place—and flattens his palm against my stomach. He groans into my mouth while he smears the liquid up to my breasts.

While my instinct is to recoil from it, Cage only fucks me harder, seeming to get off on my body being covered in it.

It should disturb me. This entire situation is beyond fucked up. Yet, it becomes impossible to feel a damn thing outside of the orgasm looming just beyond the horizon.

Cries pour from my throat, and he swallows them all, proving just how starved he is.

"Don't stop," I gasp, my voice strained. "Fuck, Cage, please."

His lips retreat from mine, trailing up along my cheek. I lose all coherent thought, my surroundings becoming disjointed and incomprehensible. The pleasure is like a disease, shutting down my nervous system and taking control. I'm a puppet to the infection, and there's nothing I can do but succumb.

Time stills, and I shatter just as he releases the belt, sending blood rushing to my head, intensifying the explosion detonating throughout my body.

My bones liquefy, and the muscles surrounding them seize. Vaguely, I feel rather than hear the broken cry leave my throat. A sound that quickly morphs into a scream when I feel something sharp bite into my face.

Directly over the scar beneath my eye.

He groans against me, flesh trapped between his teeth, and his body stills before flooding my pussy with his cum.

Burning pain battles with the euphoria rolling through me in harsh waves. It becomes so overwhelming; it feels like I'm on the verge of combusting.

"Cage!" I squeal, and finally, he releases my cheek.

The plunge back to earth is dizzying, more so when he drops his hand from the belt, allowing me to straighten.

My back aches from being in the same position for so long, so I drop forward, catching myself on both hands as I pant heavily.

Fingers brush over my back, and then his thumbs dig into my tailbone, instantly relieving some pressure.

"Jesus, way to remind me I'm not twenty-five anymore," I groan.

His soft chuckle reaches my ears, and I work up the nerve to straighten again. I cock my head over my shoulder, meeting a stare that hasn't waned in intensity.

His thumb brushes against my scar gently. "I hope you think of me next time you look in the mirror."

Insecurity rises, and I'm almost embarrassed that he's focusing on my trauma so plainly laid out on my face. I've always hated my scar, and something inside me rebels against him finding a way to make me accept it. Especially seeing as part of me wants to let him.

I narrow my eyes. "That wasn't cool. Don't do that again."

His smile widens, not the least bit ashamed.

"It didn't stop you from coming all over my cock, did it?"

"Almost."

A massive lie.

One he clearly doesn't believe by the way his lip crooks higher.

I expect a smart-ass response, but instead, he leans forward and places a kiss over the bite mark. I'm taken aback when he pulls out of me, distracting me from the surprises he keeps throwing my way. Now that I'm firmly back in reality, I'm realizing once again that I'm covered in the woman's blood.

"Let's go shower. Show me around the rest of the house while you're at it," he suggests casually.

My mouth pops open. "You—what? No. You're not coming to my house again. You haven't been invited!"

He stands and shoots me a cocky grin.

"Baby, if you keep playing hard to get, I'll fucking move in. Now, let's clean up and shower before I decide I'm hungry again."

He picks up his jeans and begins to slide them on.

And all I can do is kneel on the floor with my mouth agape and stare at his bare ass being covered.

I hate that it feels like it's too soon.

chapter nine

MOLLY

FOURTEEN YEARS AGO
2008

IT'S FUCKING HOT OUTSIDE, but even the suffocating summer air can't deter the bone-deep chill washing through me, a reaction that only standing in front of my childhood home can evoke.

The *home* I was sold from.

It's a small, yellow two-story house with missing shingles and dirty siding. It'd be considered cute and quaint in a suburb if it wasn't so broken down. If it fostered a happy family with loving parents.

However, in Reaper Canyon, a town that's seen more drug overdoses than gender reveal parties, the only thing that's been born in this shithole is half of my fucking nightmares. The other half were bred by Francesca and her filthy brother.

"This is so going to get you killed," I mutter aloud.

At any moment, my parents could stumble out the door, lay eyes on me, and call Francesca.

I'd be forced to leave Layla behind.

I don't have much of a heart left to break, but I'd give her the last piece of me if it meant she'd escape this house of horrors.

It took me two days of hitchhiking and bus rides to get here. An adventure that was almost as terrifying as escaping that house. I covered up my scar with dirt and lied to the drivers, telling them my car broke down on the way home from college, and I needed to get home to my sick mom.

By some grace of God, or Zeus, or whoever, the second driver I came across was a sweet old lady who offered me money. Enough to buy a hoodie from the thrift store, get something to eat, and take a bus the rest of the way home.

I got lucky and can only pray that it's still on my side.

Steeling my spine, I trudge through the useless, rickety chain-link fence surrounding the house, and head toward the back. My feet kick through overgrown grass that nearly reaches above my knees, the blades getting tangled around my worn shoes.

The back door leads directly into the laundry room. I can't remember the last time Mom or Dad even smelt detergent, let alone used it to clean clothes, so it's a guaranteed area of the house that they won't be in.

Dad's car is parked outside. There aren't strange cars like there usually were in the past, so I'm fairly confident they don't have any of their dirty friends over. The only thing I need to worry about is my parents seeing me before I see them.

Adrenaline courses through my bloodstream, amping my heart rate up to catastrophic levels. Eight months ago, I would've never been capable of this. Now, I don't know that I'm capable of feeling anything for anyone outside of my baby sister.

Not even for myself.

Breath stutters out of my lungs, and my lips are bone dry as I silently open the back door. I only crack it far enough to allow my body to fit through. Once it reaches the halfway point, the hinges start creaking.

The house is eerily silent, causing the hairs on my nape to stand on end. Typically, there's a TV playing cartoons in the background—for my dad's viewing pleasure, not Layla's. Or my mom screaming at the top of her lungs about what a lazy piece of shit my father is and how they have no money for their heroin because of it.

He had no problem yelling back and definitely didn't have an issue with raising his hand to her. She'd walk away with bruises, and he'd storm out the front door to go score them some more drugs, which resulted in them owing more people money.

They were dirt poor—until they sold me, of course.

Working to swallow, I creep over the pile of dirty clothes discarded haphazardly on the rotting, filthy, white linoleum floor.

I peek around the corner into the filthy kitchen. Aqua blue cupboard doors sag open, unable to close anymore. Dishes are piled in the rusting sink with flies buzzing above them, remnants of food and mold caked onto the steel and cutlery. They're also scattered across the peeling countertops, along with several opened bean and soup cans.

I balk at the awful stench. When I lived here, I grew used to it. Except now, the rot and lingering cigarette smoke bleached into the wallpaper is all I can smell. I, at least, tried to keep it clean.

Covering my nose, I make my way through the kitchen and plant myself against the wall next to the entrance of the living room.

Slowly, I peek around the corner, finding it empty. Sweat gathers along my hairline and creeps down my spine.

Everything about this scenario is unusual. And that makes me really fucking nervous.

Fuck, is Layla even here?

If she's not, I don't know what I'll do. I have no resources to find her. I have nothing.

Fucking nothing.

Panic begins to circulate into my system, a dangerous cocktail when mixed with the adrenaline.

But I can't lose my mind right now. Not yet.

"Keep it together, Molly," I whisper.

Inhaling what's supposed to be a calming breath, but is only toxic fumes, I charge through the empty living room and toward the stairs. My footsteps are silent atop the putrid green carpet covering the room, all the way up the steps and along the short hallway.

I peek into the room to my right first—Layla's nursery. It has a rickety crib inside, the cot within stained, sans a sheet, and with a threadbare blanket.

Relief overtakes me, and tears spring to my eyes, flooding my sinuses and throat until I nearly choke on them.

"Layla," I squeak, my voice splitting like dry wood.

Blonde hair spills around her like a halo while she slumbers. It's grown longer since I've last seen her. Her cheeks are still too hollow for my liking, but at least she's breathing. And right now, that's the only thing that matters.

I sniffle as I hurry toward her, praying to God she remembers me. I've been gone for eight months, which is far too long when she's so young. She's only a year old now and likely won't recognize my face anymore.

"Layla," I whisper, gently shaking her shoulder.

Long, blonde lashes splay across her cheeks, which are also paler than I'd like.

"Layla," I call again, glancing over my shoulder to ensure no one is coming.

Her eyes flutter, and then she gives me those big, beautiful blue eyes. Pretty much the only good thing that came from our mother.

"Hey, sweet baby. It's Molly. Your big sister," I coo sweetly.

She peers up at me silently, as if trying to figure out who I am. She was only four months old when I was taken, so I don't expect her to know me. I just hope she can find it in her to trust me.

"Hi, my sweet girl," I whisper, brushing away a blonde hair from her eyes.

Her arms rise, and instantly, I'm cradling her against me.

The tears bubble over, spilling down my cheeks in rivers, and it's almost impossible to breathe. I've been dreaming about this very moment for eight long, torturous months, and it almost doesn't feel real.

Like any second, I will wake up in that bed in Francesca's house, Rocco breathing over me.

Just like that, I'll lose her again.

I don't know if I'd survive it.

"Da da da da," she blabbers quietly.

"Shh, baby, we gotta be—"

"I knew you were going to show your ugly face here."

The sharp voice is like a whip cracking against my back. My spine snaps straight, and I pivot on my heel quick enough to cause me to stumble.

My heart hammers painfully against my chest as I take in the source of all my pain. The man who was supposed to love me but could only ever hurt me. And one of the last faces I saw before that cloth covered my mouth, and I woke up in a nightmare worse than anything my brain could conjure up.

"Hey, Dad," I greet nervously, the tremor in my voice betraying how terrified I am.

He takes a menacing step forward, prompting me to retreat immediately.

His gray, greasy hairs stand haphazardly on end, and though his eyes are full of hatred and disbelief, it's clear he's just woken up. He's wearing his dirty button-up work shirt, with *Raymond* stitched onto the left breast pocket.

He's a mechanic, and *of course,* it's time for him to go to work.

"W-where's Mom?" I choke out, my gaze ping-ponging between his menacing stare and the hallway behind him.

His lip curls. "Dead."

I blink, more shocked by his declaration than I expected. Maybe because she's survived so much abuse from my father and other men, it seemed like she was indestructible. Or because there were so many nights where I laid awake, praying for her death, and it never came.

I'm surprised.

But not fucking sad.

"How?"

"Overdose."

"Let me guess, from the drugs you bought with all the money you made from selling me?" I snap.

His grin is full of intentions as rotten and black as his teeth.

"Died a couple weeks ago. Dumb bitch got too excited and injected herself with some strong shit we ain't ever had before," he clips. Then, he chuckles, the sound raspy and wet. "And now you're back. Rocco called yesterday lookin' for ya. Promised me 'nother fifty-K if I let him know when you showed up."

My heart drops, another shot of panic torpedoing through my insides, landing in the pit of dread welling in my stomach.

I need to get the fuck out of here *now*.

"Whad'ya do? Give 'em bad sex or som'n'?" he asks nastily.

I narrow my eyes. I can't even be insulted. He talks as if it was my choice to be enslaved and groomed to be sold to a disgusting sick fuck. Like I did the family a fucking favor.

"Ya know, I may not call 'im. I might just have to find me some different people this time 'round. Police have been investigatin' me. Think I had somethin' to do with that whole shitshow with you in the gas station." A loud laugh bursts out of him. "Did you know they can wipe people from security footage? Don't know what kind of genius they got on their hands, but they made you look fuckin' crazy. Me and Louis weren't even in 'em! Every day I turn on the news, they're talkin' 'bout you running from ghosts."

My mouth drops while he cackles loudly. They wiped my kidnappers from the footage? I had hoped to God those cameras were recording, only it feels like a punch to the gut to hear that they manipulated it.

"Only reason they're on my ass is 'cause of that fucking asshole clerk making a statement against me. I'd hoped they'd kill his ass, too, but they said it'd cost me since he ain't got nothin' on us. And, well, he looks just as crazy as you, so he ain't worth the cash. Police don't have shit on me." He ends that statement with a smart-ass grin.

"They will," I spit through clenched teeth. "You fucking sold me!"

Layla huddles into my neck, upset by the obvious tension between Dad and me. I bounce her in my arms, hoping to keep her calm, yet knowing it's likely useless.

"You was useless around here anyway! Tryna steal mine and your mom's baby. That's all you cared about. Layla, Layla, Layla. That's where all your money went instead of paying us rent. Just spendin' our money and living here for free!"

An argument forms on my tongue, building to a monument as tall as fucking Giza, but it's not worth it.

I need to get me and Layla out of here as soon as possible before my father makes good on his promise and calls Rocco here. Or someone worse.

"The only person you have to worry about is yourself," I hiss. "Layla and I will be gone."

Another step, and his face morphs from barely human to demonic.

"As far as I see it, she's still in my custody. Which means she goes where *I* want her to go. You were a pretty penny in my pocket the first time, but you two together? I'll get a fuck of a lot more, no?"

My upper lip curls in disgust, and a hatred unlike anything I've felt before consumes me. It's so potent that the only way for my body to process it is to shake violently.

It's not just wrath.

It's pure fucking murderous rage.

To sell me is one thing.

But to sell a *baby?*

I have no words for how fucking evil that is. No words to describe how decrepit a soul must be to condemn a child so willingly in such a horrific way.

My vision grows spotty with fury, and I set Layla down in the crib as calmly as possible. She lets out a cry of protest, raising her arms and squeezing her tiny hands for me to pick her up again.

"I'll be right here, baby. It's okay," I assure her gently, even though my words tremble.

That doesn't soothe her. But more than anything, I need to get this vile man away from her.

She doesn't deserve to witness what I plan on doing to him. No child should ever see that.

"Let's go downstairs and discuss this. Otherwise, I'll call Rocco myself and tell him you kidnapped me back."

He scoffs out a laugh. "You think they'll believe that?"

"You're right," I agree mockingly. "You're too stupid. I'll tell them I escaped, and you tried selling me off to another fucking pedophile ring. They'll still take us, then they'll kill you, too."

Suddenly, his mouth twists into a scathing snarl. He glances up and down my form, his muddy brown eyes filled with loathing. Silently, he jerks his head toward the hallway, then stalks off toward the staircase.

"I'll be right back, pretty girl," I murmur absently, white noise flooding my brain.

There is no clear thought in my head, just a loud ringing. Woodenly, I follow him, gently shutting Layla's door behind me. I'm not sure if she can climb out of her crib or not, but she's still too little to reach the doorknob. She won't be able to get out.

I reach the top of the steps and stare down them blankly, understanding that he's waiting for me and what this discussion is going to come down to, yet unable to find a conscience to stop myself.

I exhale and make my way down the stairs, finding my dad waiting in the kitchen. He's leaning against the counter, sipping out of the same mug he's always drank out of. Coffee and a shot of Jack Daniels.

"Your mom used to make me lunch for work. Gotta admit, I miss 'er for that, at least," he comments casually, finishing with a chuckle.

He's pretending that we will be engaging in a civil conversation, but he's as tense as I am. He thinks he's going to win, and for the second time in my life, I'll wake up in the back of a stranger's van.

This time, with my baby sister beside me.

"What is it you think you're goin' to do, hm?" he questions, amusement glimmering in his dead eyes. "You think you can hurt me?"

He laughs while I edge toward a tiny round table in the corner of the room, where Mom used to sit every morning, smoking a cigarette and drinking her own coffee and whiskey.

"I think I've faced men far scarier than you and survived."

"You sure about that?" he challenges.

His smile dims, and his gaze slides over to the scar beneath my eye. The very one he gave me when I was ten years old.

I remember that night vividly. Back then, he still had teeth, and he lost his mind to whatever drug he injected into his veins.

He left them all over my body when he raped me.

He, on the other hand, has no recollection of it. If it wasn't for my mom bearing witness to it, he'd be convinced it was someone else. She was also drugged and too delirious to stop him.

Afterward, when Dad attempted to deny it, that was the only moment Mom stood up for me by screaming at him for hurting me. Not because I was assaulted, but because she'd have to explain the bite on my face to the school. The others covering my body could be hidden, just not that one.

Later, she spit on me for trying to steal her husband. As if he wasn't my own father.

Ultimately, it became the result of a play date gone wrong with a nonexistent cousin who had aggression issues. Despite that, it didn't look like a kid's bite; the school believed them, and it was never addressed again.

I cock my head, leaning against the table behind me and resting my linked hands on top. "Do you think a bite to the face is the worst thing that's been done to me? I've lived through so much worse, *Dad*."

He sets his cup on the crowded countertop, and his features slacken into a monstrous expression. Chin dropped, mouth hanging open, and an evil glare beneath his eyebrows.

"Not yet, ya haven't," he threatens darkly.

He edges toward me casually, as if he isn't planning my death. Not by his hands, of course. But by the highest bidder's. While he snorts, smokes, and injects the only form of happiness he's ever felt. Until escaping reality becomes eternal.

Just like it did with Mom.

Behind me sits her discarded mug. It's likely been there since she died—forgotten.

Just like her.

I'd like to think this is Mom extending the hand she never extended when she was alive. A peace offering, maybe.

Subtly, I loop my finger through the handle, and he pauses a few feet away. Right out of arm's length, making me sigh.

If only she gave that much of a shit.

Time stands still, except for the consistent beat inside my chest, reminding me that I'm still alive. I'm still fighting.

Then, he lunges, and I'm swinging, the mug in my hand cracking against his temple. Ceramic shatters, and a shard cuts into my palm.

He roars, and his arm swings out wildly, attempting to grab ahold of me. But if there's one thing I learned about people with more artificial chemicals in their bodies than blood—they have no fucking aim.

I duck and tackle him to the floor while he's unbalanced, the back of his head smacking off it harshly. A curse flies out of his mouth and he's grappling to get a leg up so he can flip me over. But I'm already on top of him, a piece of the mug gripped between my fingers and pressed against his jugular.

It only lasts half a second, and he's carelessly knocking away my hand before sending a fist flying toward my face. Just barely, I flinch to the side, his knuckles clipping my cheek and sending a shooting pain throughout my face.

But my desperation outweighs the sting, and I'm rushing to get my knees over his biceps. Several times, he deters me, nearly throwing me off just for me to crawl back onto him. Finally, I send my own fist into his nose, allowing me to stun him long enough to get his arms pinned beneath my knees, putting all my weight onto him.

I press the piece back into his jugular again, the shard having already shredded my own skin from the struggle.

"Make one fucking move, and I'll slit your throat, asshole," I spit through heavy pants.

My hand trembles against him, my vision narrowing until all I see is his disgusting face, contorted in rage with gray scruff covering his jaw.

"You're a pathetic man," I snarl. "And there isn't a single soul on this planet that will care when you're gone."

He laughs, and his rotten breath fans across my face. I dig the sharp end deeper, a bead of blood blooming from the tip.

"That don't matter to me, baby. Come on, you know better than that. Even if I was a fucking stand-up citizen, I'd go down in history like everybody else. Forgotten. My name carved in some stupid gravestone that people pass by and don't look twice at. And ya know what? The same thing will happen to you."

"Yeah, you're right," I say, my voice breathless and trembling. "But at least when I go down, I'll be able to say I took as many of you sick fucks as I could with me."

Another full belly laugh releases from his throat, though the desperation is evident. He doesn't want to die, and at any moment, he's going to renew his fight.

So, I make a quick decision and slice the opposite side of his throat. He'll bleed out eventually, but it won't be over before I'm ready.

His eyes widen, and his mouth flops while he chokes on his own blood. Blood that spurts onto my face, neck, and chest.

"Fucking bitch!"

Uncaring, I lean forward until his eyes find their way to mine, his pupils little pinpoints.

I shake my head. "No. You don't get the privilege of seeing me while you die."

Dropping the ceramic, I cup his face between my palms and place my thumbs over his eyes.

"No, no, no!" he shouts, though the words are garbled. His fingers wrap around my wrists, attempting to pull them away. But the blood loss has made him weak, and he fails miserably.

It takes a few seconds of pushing until I feel his eyes pop. His answering scream is loud, broken, and full of agony. It's a sound I've grown accustomed to with other girls in Francesca's house. Before, it shattered my heart when I heard it. Now, I feel nothing.

Crimson puddles in the craters of his pulverized eyes, flooding my hands, and down either side of his face. A sea of red.

I chuckle aloud. "Moses probably wouldn't appreciate me calling your face the Red Sea, huh?" I laugh again, the sound hoarse and broken. "Then again, he probably isn't appreciating any of this."

I don't stop until I've smashed them into his puny brain and his struggles cease.

The earth got a little cleaner today.

His hands drop from my arms, and as he goes completely limp, so do I. I just... deflate. Like his eyeballs, I suppose.

That thought wrings another tired giggle out of me.

I'm covered in blood, sweat, and probably other shit I don't want to know about. My heart is racing, and my lungs are incredibly tight.

Killing... killing is *a lot* of fucking work.

Then, my thoughts spiral, and panic overtakes me. How the fuck am I going to cover this up?

"Shit," I whisper, dropping my head.

Thankfully, the neighbors are drug addicts, too, and there were many nights when they were in screaming matches that rivaled Mom and Dad's. Our struggle shouldn't raise any of their concerns, and even if it did, I doubt they'd be kind enough to call the police.

As for his job, it's not unusual for Dad to not show up without warning. He's lost many jobs over the years, primarily due to him going on binges. Sometimes for weeks at a time. They might call for a week, but eventually, they'll give up.

Same for his friends—they don't bother coming over unless he's offering them drugs.

Raymond Devereaux doesn't have anyone that actually gives a shit about him.

But he is in the public eye now.

Francesca used to turn on the TV and show me all the news reports and search parties after I was kidnapped. She would laugh and laugh about how many people were looking for me.

"Look at aaalll those people. And not a single one will find you."

She found that funny.

And now, I need to ensure that's exactly what happens. They can never find me. They can never know I came back here.

That couple—Latoya and Devin—might talk to the media. Claim they had me in their house. But they'll never be able to prove it, and eventually, speculation will become just that.

"No evidence," I whisper. "There can't be any evidence."

My DNA is all over this house. Finding pieces of my hair or fingerprints on every surface wouldn't be out of the ordinary.

However, on a dead body? That would be catastrophic.

I inhale deeply and then release it slowly, feeling my brain switch off once more.

No one is looking for him yet. I have time to clean up, get Layla situated, and then dispose of his body.

After, I'll take Layla out of here and never look back.

"What to do with you," I wonder aloud, heading for the limited cleaning supplies beneath the sink, racking my brain and trying to remember the crime documentaries I've seen Mom watch and if any of them ever talked about getting rid of a body.

"Melting him?" I ask myself under my breath. "No. Too messy, and I don't even know the proper chemicals. Can't bury him or put him in a lake. That *always* gets people caught."

My mind turns over idea after idea while I wrap his body in garbage bags, rejecting them all for one reason or another.

And just as I begin to scrub the floor, I remember one episode I had seen. A proverbial light bulb illuminates, and I pause as I think it over.

"Pig farm," I whisper, a slight grin curling my lips.

And I know just where to find one.

chapter ten

MOLLY

PRESENT
2022

"IF I WOULD'VE KNOWN that you were going to throw yourself all over me in the shower, I would've directed you to the guest bathroom," I mutter, pulling a clean white tank top over my head.

He cocks a brow, unimpressed. "At which point did I give the indication that I'd keep my hands to myself? We'll play it back, and I'll redo that part so you're not confused anymore."

I roll my eyes.

"I'm not confused," I deny vehemently, shooting him an annoyed look.

Yet, I am.

I'm confused *and* a fucking liar.

He wears only his boxers—pretty much the only article of clothing that didn't get dirty. His shirt is a lost cause, leaving him with his black jeans and leather jacket, but regardless, he'll likely go home smelling like a pigpen. It takes a special kind of soap to get it out, but I won't divulge that information, purely because I'm irritated with him.

Even more, I'm angry he's not a sensible person who carries extra clothes on hand. His body is downright distracting, making it extremely hard to remember why I'm annoyed.

Right. Because he fucked me in the shower again and reminded me that sex can actually be... *so* good. It took years to forget that after the first time we met. And now I've relapsed and become addicted all over again.

Fucker.

Keeping my back to him, I pump a few dollops of lotion into my hand and start slathering it over my hands, arms, and chest. His eyes are like two little lasers burning into me, but I do my best to ignore him.

It was just sex.

That's it.

"You're about to kick me out," he surmises from behind me. I jump, not expecting his voice to be right at my goddamn back.

"What else would we do? Play ponies and have a pillow fight?" I snap.

I sound defensive. I *am* defensive.

Tension is clustered in my muscles like it has nowhere else to go.

Gritting my teeth, I sit on the edge of the bed and force myself to meet his probing stare. It's not angry like I had expected. Or annoyed, even. No. He looks fucking amused.

He bends at the knees, lowering himself until I'm peering down at him with an incredulous stare.

"I've been dying to know who you are, Molly. Is that so wrong?"

Is he fucking with me? It's incredibly wrong. It's literally the worst thing he could ask me for. To *know* me? That would be willingly inviting him into my life, and I've made damn sure to turn my insides into a crowded room, with no space for anyone.

"Yes," I bite. "You know what my pussy feels like wrapped around you. That's more than most could say. At least, those who are still alive."

He hums, and a darkness passes over his green eyes, turning them into a shadowy, dreary forest. "So, you're telling me that there are others out there who have this knowledge and are still breathing?"

A few months ago, after finally feeling ready to face them after all these years, I had asked Legion to investigate the men in that house and see if any were still alive. After researching, he'd said all of them were dead. Except one.

Kenny Mathers.

He's very rich and well-protected. Unlike most buyers who came around only for the Culling, he frequented the house often.

I overheard Francesca telling Rocco that Kenny was interested in buying me specifically, which is why he couldn't seem to stay away. From the house, and from me.

His money and elitism have kept him safe all these years, allowing him to go off-grid altogether. He hasn't been seen in the public eye since not long after I escaped.

Admittedly, I hadn't been ready to face him, though I did make Legion aware of who he was and what he did. If my boss has done anything about it, I'm not sure. I've been too chickenshit to ask.

"Only one that I know of, but who even knows if that's still the case. Regardless, don't kill anyone on my behalf. Fucking me a few times doesn't make you my hero."

He cocks his head, appearing unfazed by my demand. "What's his name?"

I sigh. "Why does it matter?"

His expression is serious, not an iota of amusement remaining in his stare.

"I want to be the only man on this entire fucking planet that knows what you feel like. And if I'm sharing this knowledge with a single soul still walking this earth, then I will be removing them from it."

I can only blink at him, speechless for a few beats. Despite that, my stomach is a cesspool of restless butterflies, and I feel my heart beginning to soften.

His words aren't terrifying—but my reaction is.

"You're being ridiculous."

"I could be."

"You're not killing anyone on my behalf."

"I will."

"I'm not arguing with you about this, Cage."

"Then don't."

I sigh again, my shoulders slumping. I'm emotionally spent for the night, and I have no energy to convince him to keep his murdering hands to himself.

The prospect of him killing the remaining man from Francesca's house doesn't bother me—but his reasoning does. I don't want him to do it for *me*. Because he harbors any type of emotion for me. I'd rather he just snuff him out from the planet for being a monster and leave it at that.

"What is it you want from me?" I groan, sliding my hand down my face in exasperation.

"As many pieces as you're willing to give for the night."

I drop my hand and gape at him blankly, but he only waits patiently, gazing up at me.

"I just want to know about you. That's all. I'll tell you anything you want to know, too."

I twist my lips, feeling myself relent. Mostly because I'm undeniably curious about Cage, too. I spent many lone nights in Alaska wondering about the man who completely obliterated my world with so much ease. What bothered me most was that I missed him. How could I miss someone I don't even know?

I'm hoping that if I give him what he wants, he'll find something entirely unlikable and want to go home. Then, I can finally go to bed. *Alone.*

I can't afford my world being decimated again, and this time, I won't have to miss him.

"My favorite name in the world is Layla."

My throat tightens, and I curse myself for saying her name. It's impossible to think about her without feeling like my heart is being pushed through a woodchipper. I should've given him something impersonal. Like my favorite color.

He nods slowly, and the tiniest of grins curls one side of his lips upward. God, that look is lethal. I hate it.

"It's beautiful."

"Yep," I croak, then clear my throat, a pathetic attempt to cover the emotion clogging my windpipe.

"My favorite flower is a tiger lily," he tells me. Hesitantly, I meet his gaze again, but this time, I see shadows within them. "My mother was a single mom, and my father died before I was born. Growing up, she would buy herself tiger lilies every Saturday at the farmers' market. She said she didn't need a man because she could get herself anything she wanted. When I got my first paycheck, that was the first thing I bought her. I told her she may not need a man to buy them for her, but that doesn't mean she doesn't deserve it."

"Let me guess—you never stopped buying them for her," I say, a smile involuntarily curling my lips.

He grins, and my heart turns into putty. "Still do."

Goddamn him.

He was supposed to tell me something that made me find him abhorrent. Absolutely vile.

But then, his smile drops, and his features rearrange into an expression that instantly feels daunting. I already know what he's thinking. I can see it written all over his face.

"Let me guess," I repeat, my voice barely above a whisper. "You want to talk about my kidnapping."

"I knew who you were before you walked into my store. The whole world did. And, like most people, I was obsessed with your case. The security footage..."

"Made me look crazy," I supply, my stomach filling with acid.

"I know technology well, and it was clear that it was manipulated. You weren't crazy, and I understood that not only was the worst moment of your life broadcasted to the entire world, but that they altered it to make you look a certain way. Even back then, I was angry for you."

"Thanks," I mutter bitterly. "Is that why you fucked me? Wanted to play with the famous missing girl and have bragging rights?"

His face slackens, and he appears disappointed.

"No, Molly. The only person I ever told was Silas, and only because I was fucking hammered. And I fucked you because I was attracted to you in a way I've never felt for anyone else. I think I became obsessed with your case because my soul recognized yours. And I had so many questions about you."

"Did you get your answers?" I ask, my tone hardening. I'm looking for reasons to be mad, but truthfully, I can't blame him for knowing about my kidnapping or being intrigued by it. The video footage is... it's something that most *couldn't* ignore.

The girl who seemed to disappear out of thin air.

And the girl who was chased by ghosts. Little did they know, I *am* the ghost.

"Not the ones that matter, which is why I want to know you, Molly. I want to know the girl that the world still thinks is dead."

"I *like* it that way," I clip. "Everyone is too involved in their own lives to recognize a missing girl from fifteen years ago. This means I don't become a pony for the media circus, and I'm left alone. There's a reason I haven't let anyone get to know me."

He nods, and the gentle look in his eyes is what makes me realize I'm beginning to freak out a little. My heart is racing, my palms sweaty.

"I'm not going to tell anyone," he assures. "I'm too selfish to share you with anyone, let alone fucking vultures that would risk your safety. I would never put you in danger."

I exhale a heavy breath, attempting to release the anxiety that has begun to poison my bloodstream.

"There's a possibility that I'd be a suspect in a murder if the media learned I did escape." He stays quiet, letting me gather the courage to confess something I've never told a single soul. "When I escaped, I went back to my parents' house. I have a sister, and she was only a year old at the time. I couldn't leave her with the people who had sold me for drug money."

His upper lip twitches, fury settling in his gaze. I don't know why, but that invigorates me to keep going.

"My mom had already died of an overdose, so it was just my father. When he saw that I was back, he talked about selling me again, but this time, Layla, too. And I just... snapped. I couldn't handle the thought of him selling my baby sister. The things I had gone through—all I could think about was those same things happening to Layla—" I cut myself off, too overwhelmed with the thought. That residual fury resurfaces, and my cheeks grow hot as my words turn flustered.

His hand grabs mine, and I focus on it, if only to distract me from my spiraling thoughts.

While I had seen they were covered in tattoos, it's the first time I've actually gotten to study them closely. He tattooed flames on the knuckles of his fingers, the background behind them blacked out to give the illusion that they're melting candles. The artwork is some of the best I've seen, and for the first time, I consider getting my scars covered up with something beautiful.

"So you killed him," he states, bringing me back to the conversation.

"I killed him," I confirm quietly. "And I didn't even feel guilty about it."

"You shouldn't have," he says. "He deserved that and so much worse."

I nod. He did, and there's some satisfaction in knowing that I had been the one to end his life.

"I had heard about a large pig farm a couple hours from where I used to live. The owner was a local source of meat for many people, and there had been talk that he would be retiring soon. So, I cleaned everything up, rolled my dad in garbage bags, and put him in the trunk of his car."

He cocks a brow. "Would I happen to have just fucked you at the same farm?"

A blush immediately blooms across my cheeks. Damn it.

Clearing my throat, I mutter, "Yes."

He grins, and I narrow my eyes at the satisfaction emanating from him.

"Anyway," I continue, shooting him a pointed *shut up* look. "Once I got Layla and I showered, dressed, and packed, I drove to the farm. I waited until the owner went to bed, snuck into his barn, and fed my father to his pigs. It wasn't pretty, and I didn't do everything right. That was how I learned pigs avoided teeth and hair, which made the cleanup process awful. I'm still surprised I managed to get away with it."

It's a grossly oversimplified version of that night, but it's the crux of it. The details don't really matter now, except that I've learned a lot about feeding people to pigs since then. Most importantly, I had successfully gotten Layla and me away from that house, and no one has identified who we truly are since.

"Where's Layla now?"

I twist my lips in an attempt to keep my chin from trembling. That question feels like a sucker punch to the chest. My heart squeezes painfully, and a deep sadness consumes me.

"Emma," I correct. "Her name is Emma now. Four years is how long I tried to take care of her. Since my dad was under investigation for my disappearance, it didn't take long for the feds to notice him and Layla missing. She was broadcast all over the news, just as I was, and there were so many conspiracies about what happened to the three of us. Some people speculated that I escaped and took her, but there was never enough evidence to support it.

"So, I renamed her Emma, and I tried *so* hard to take care of her. It was almost impossible to get a job because I couldn't get an ID and expose myself. I managed to find a few under-the-table jobs, though they were typically underpaid, and my bosses somehow managed to be a shit person every time. It wasn't sustainable, and I wasn't providing a safe, healthy life for her."

A rock forms in my throat and for a moment, I can't breathe, let alone speak. Ten years isn't nearly long enough to smooth away the pain and devastation. A lifetime wouldn't even be enough.

Cage flexes his hand around mine again, reminding me he's here.

"I found a nice family in a wealthy town, and I stalked the fuck out of them. I watched them for months, ensuring they were good—*truly* good people with happy kids. And then... once I was positive they'd be able to give her the life she deserved... I waited until she fell asleep, then left her on their doorstep with a name tag and her birthdate like she was a goddamn dog."

My eyes flood with tears, and even as my chest heaves and my lungs expand, it still feels like I can't fucking breathe.

"I continued to watch them for several months afterward to make sure they actually took her in and didn't give her to some foster home. It took a little while, but eventually, they were able to adopt her. Since she was older than when I first took her and several hours away from our hometown, no one suspected who she was. Plus, I made sure she only ever knew me by Marie. It was chalked up to a druggie mother who just left their kid on a stranger's doorstep. And I was okay with that. It meant she was safe and could finally live in some goddamn peace."

Everything burns—my wet eyes, nose, cheeks, and throat.

"When Legion found me, it had been a year since I dropped her off. I never saw him, but he must've seen me when my boss was getting aggressive with me. He sent me to you, and the rest is history."

I bounce my leg anxiously, the urge to cry becoming harder to contain. "Fuck, it still sucks that I couldn't provide for her," I choke out, my voice broken with tears.

"But you did provide," he insists, catching ahold of my wandering gaze. "That option was stolen from you, baby. It's not because you weren't capable, but because you were in danger just as much as her. You were young. And I know it's not your home she's sleeping in. However, you *did* provide her with the life she deserves. *You* gave her that."

I squeeze my eyes shut, a few tears wiggling free anyway.

"I'm selfish and want her to remember me like I do her. But I know that I'll never be able to be in her life. Not with my lifestyle. I want her to stay far away from this shit. But I missed her so much when I was in Alaska. I was a fucking zombie, no matter how hard I tried to live."

My lungs are still tight, yet I force myself to keep going, even though it feels like each word is made of fiberglass.

"So, four years ago, I broke down and moved back. The previous owner had passed, and the farm had been up for sale for a while. I had a decent job in Alaska and used all my savings to buy it. I feel better being in the same state as Layla, even if I can't be in her life."

I end my explanation with a sigh, feeling exhausted suddenly. Emotionally and physically. I hadn't planned on telling him that much, though admittedly, it felt good. But now, I just want to sleep.

"Do you still watch her?" Cage asks boldly. My eyes drop to my lap, where I fidget with my fingers. A flush crawls up my throat, embarrassment taking root.

"Yes," I admit, forcing volume into my voice. Maybe it's wrong or creepy, but she's my sister and I care too much not to check up on her. And while it's a tad embarrassing, I also don't feel guilty about it, either.

He chuckles. "I'd do the same if the roles were reversed."

I smile tiredly, on the verge of resting my head on the pillow and passing out, even if he doesn't leave. Letting him stay one night doesn't have to be a big deal.

Once more, he squeezes my hand, drawing my attention back down to him.

"You saved her life, Molly. Remember that. Always remember that."

chapter eleven

MOLLY

NINE YEARS AGO
2013

"*Jesus*, YOU'RE SO FUCKING sexy. When did Brent hire you? If I had known, I'd have visited my cousin sooner and already have you naked in my bed."

He's definitely an incel. I can't imagine a remark like that working on a single woman when he's missing his two front teeth and his pale skin is pinkened and covered in scabs from drug use.

I lean heavily on the counter separating us, staring at him like he's a fly that's expecting me to be impressed with its crooked wings when it has shit smeared across its upper lip.

"Please tell me, how many women have you successfully gotten in your bed with that pickup line?"

He grins, accentuating the blond peach fuzz peppered above his mouth. I bet he thinks it makes him look more like a man.

"I got one in there right now. But I'll gladly kick her out just for you."

Disgusting.

I hate this fucking job. I hate my boss. And evidently, I hate his family, too.

I've been working in this god-awful mechanic shop for a month and have been sexually harassed more times than I can count. I'm at my wit's end, but I need the money.

"No, thanks," I quip. "I'll let Brent know you're here to see him."

His smile falls, replaced with a dark expression. I give him my back before something foul falls out of his mouth—worse than what already has.

The small shop is nestled in a run-down town deep in the mountains of Montana. Luckily, I haven't seen my face plastered anywhere here, and the media has moved on to another world event that only affirms this planet has gone to hell.

Now that I no longer have Layla, I wonder why I even bother walking amongst the living. But I refuse to have fought so hard for my life just to throw it away. I can only call it pure stubbornness at this point.

"Brent, your cousin is here," I call into his office, standing firmly outside the door. Every time I go in, he asks me to shut it behind me, and it always ends in a highly uncomfortable situation. Most times, he hits on me. Other times, he finds a reason to berate me, then tops it off with a lovely threat.

He knows I'm running from something since I admitted it's too dangerous for me to have a driver's license, and he loves to use that as collateral.

"Which one?"

"He didn't say," I respond woodenly.

He sighs, the sound laced with irritation.

"Then how do I know he's my cousin?" he snaps. "You know damn well I got the police up my ass. And the first one goin' under the bus is *you*, little girl."

And there's the threat.

"I'll go ask," I mumble.

He mutters an insult beneath his breath while I trudge back toward the creep. He's fiddling with the car scents, taking one off the rack, sniffing it, and deliberately returning it to the wrong row, all the while wearing a smart-ass smirk on his ugly face. I clench my teeth, anger flaring. Brent's yelled at me several times for not having the scents arranged correctly when customers do exactly that.

"What's your name?" I ask, attempting to keep my expression neutral. Last thing I want him to know is that his endeavor to piss me off is working.

His answering grin is evil, and I hate the way that makes me want to retreat in on myself. I've seen that very face far too often. And what comes after.

"You need my social security card, too? Just get my fucking cousin."

It takes effort to refrain from spitting on him the way he just spit on me. Keeping the saliva in his mouth with that gap must be impossible.

"He wants your name first," I insist.

"I ain't doing shit— Brent! Brent, get the fuck out here!" he yells loudly.

Fuck.

My heart speeds as I hear my boss's door slam shut behind him, followed by his angry footfalls. Panic unleashes, and I'm assaulted by the memories of Rocco charging at me with the same heavy steps.

Brent stomps up to the cash register, fire in his brown eyes. Sweat gathers along my hairline while I fight to stay in the present. Except, I don't know that reality is much better.

"The fuck you yellin' for?" he snaps, glaring at the man for a beat, before turning it onto me. This time, I do shrink away.

My boss is a big man. And he's *mean.*

Distantly, I hear the chime of another customer entering the shop, though none of us acknowledge them.

"This little bitch refused to get you after I asked nicely. She's fucking disrespectful!"

Being called a bitch is certainly nothing new and certainly doesn't hurt my feelings, but him risking my job is absolutely uncalled for.

My mouth falls open, a protest building on my tongue. However, it instantly dissipates when Brent's accusing stare swings onto me.

"That true?"

"I-I was just trying to get his name like you asked," I defend myself weakly.

"Bullshit. She was fucking grilling me, man!"

"Shut up, Bud," Brent barks, though he keeps his fiery gaze on mine.

The familiarity between the two is apparent. Guess that means he is Brent's cousin, which only makes my situation worse.

"Go into my office and wait for me," he orders darkly.

The intention in his eyes is unmistakable. If I do as he says, I'll be walking out with one less piece of myself intact.

I nod, the movement jerky, as I turn toward his office. There's also an exit this way, and if I want to save myself, then it's imperative I take it.

Another job bites the dust, and I still have little money to show for it.

Devastation mingles with my growing anxiety. I'll have to find another town and beg for an illegal job, yet again. And the likelihood of finding a boss who's a decent human being is low. I haven't had one thus far and have gone through four jobs now.

I'm exhausted. So fucking exhausted.

"The dumb bitch can't even arrange these right," his cousin—Bud—snaps. "The strawberry is mixed with the..."

I don't hear the rest of what he says, and I don't need to. He only cemented the necessity to get the fuck out of here.

I speed-walk directly toward the exit and charge out of there without a backward glance. Sunlight pierces my eyes, though I hardly register the sharp pain. I have tunnel vision, and the only thing on my mind is getting as far away from *Engines & Oil* as possible.

By the time I reach the bus stop, I've no idea how much time has passed. I don't remember a single second of it, nor the entire ride to the women's shelter I've been staying at.

With clouded thoughts, I eventually make it to the shelter. There aren't many women boarded here, thankfully, but I am required to have group therapy sessions with them to stay.

It's incredibly uncomfortable. At least they're like me here, traumatized, and just want to be left alone. And it helps I get my own little apartment, though I am required to pay a small fee to keep it. The shelter's meant to give survivors a form of independence away from their abusers, and it's considerably cheaper than renting regular apartments around the area.

I reach my door and nearly shove through it to get inside, convinced Brent followed me and is right behind me. Though I didn't see a single soul, it still feels like someone was right on my tail the entire way home.

Only when the door is shut and locked do I throw myself against it and release a heavy exhale.

I'm incapable of feeling relieved when I'm in near-constant danger, but at least I'm not alone in that office with Brent, possibly on the brink of being assaulted again.

That... that's honestly all I could ask for at this very moment. That, and to not have been followed home by one of those creeps.

Another exhale, and then a sob is bursting free. I slap a hand over my mouth, yet it's a hopeless attempt to contain the outcry.

Soon, I'm overcome with them, and I'm no longer capable of standing. I slide down the door, my shoulders shaking and chest heaving as wail after wail rebounds against my palm.

Tears stream down my cheeks in rivers, and for the longest while, there's no thought behind my agony.

I'm not even sure why I'm crying anymore. Because of what could've happened? Or because I have to start over once again? Maybe it's because no matter how hard I try to get my feet firmly beneath me, they always get kicked out.

I just... I can't *take* this anymore.

I don't want to die, but I don't want to exist. And I wish with every ounce of my soul that I was never born. That I had never been brought into a world so cold, violent, and full of heartache.

And the worst part is that even though I feel dead inside, I'm painfully aware of how alive I am. I dread every night when I fall asleep because I know I have to wake up again and do this life for another day.

I just don't want to be here. That's all I want.

The sobs wane, but the tears are constant. Snot leaks down my nose no matter how hard I sniff, and eventually, my butt begins to ache from sitting on the unforgiving tile for so long.

Forcing my eyes open, I glance around at my abysmal home. The small cube of stained white tile around the front door transitions into a thin brown carpet. The walls are freshly painted white, though it doesn't bring much light into the dark room.

Unlike the house I grew up in, it doesn't reek of cigarette smoke, body fluids, and grime. It's just old. And it's the nicest home I've ever had. But it's still not mine.

Which is why I kept it bare, save for the standard furniture that came with it. No decorations. No personality. No... life.

Sighing, I wipe away the tears and force myself to stand. Group therapy isn't until later, but they usually set out a tray of sweets beforehand. At this moment, a chocolate brownie is the only thing I have to look forward to.

I blink away the residual wetness in my eyes, then peek through the eyehole to ensure no creepy ex-bosses or cousins are outside. Once I'm confident the coast is clear, I unlock the door and swing it open. Something black and sturdy clinks to the ground, and my heart instantly drops.

A journalist found me. Or a stranger that's planning on reporting me to the police. Different scenarios shuttle through my brain at lightning speed. Where they saw me. If they're waiting somewhere for me.

How long do I have to escape? Or is it too late?

It feels as if I'm having a heart attack as I shakily bend over and grab the card. It's metal, which surprises me first. Then, I flip it over to find the word *Legion* in bold, gold-foiled letters. Below is a phone number and nothing else.

No real name. No job title. Nothing.

But they look really fucking important.

Heart in my throat, I glance around suspiciously, still seeing no one, but not trusting that in the slightest. Other apartments surround the shelter, and the street is directly to my right. There are many places for them to hide.

Quickly, I retreat into my apartment and slam the door shut, relocking it again. Then, I distractedly make my way to my bed and slump down on the edge of it.

What the fuck is *Legion?* And what could they possibly want with me?

For a good five minutes, I argue with myself. To call them or run like my life depends on it and hope to God this *Legion* never finds me again. It doesn't look like a business card for a journalist or government official. And part of me is aware that if either one of those people found me, they'd be knocking on that door, not leaving me some obscure, ominous card.

Plus, it's incredibly fancy. It screams money.

I'm fairly confident a cop or news reporter doesn't make *this* much cash. Not enough to justify wasting it on a card, anyway.

I growl, growing irritated with myself. Without further thought, I slide my prepaid flip phone out of my back pocket, dial the number, and press call before I can talk myself out of it.

Curiosity won, and like a cat, it may get me killed.

The ringing stops, replaced by a sinfully delicious voice. Deep and raspy, yet toneless.

"I was hoping you'd call."

My lips part, so incredibly unprepared that I'm at a loss for words.

Oddly, he waits. Doesn't even question if I'm still on the line.

After a few moments, I get my shit together long enough to eke out, "Who is this?"

"Legion," he answers simply.

"And what do you want? How did you find me?" My tone grows increasingly aggressive with each word, the gears in my brain switching from shock to suspicion.

"I saw you at the mechanic and witnessed what transpired between you and your boss. You looked like someone who needed help, so I followed you home. Of course, I didn't want to make you feel more unsafe than I already have, so I let you decide to make contact."

I blink, unable to formulate a single coherent thought.

"Would you like my help?" he asks evenly.

"I— What does that entail?"

"A new life where you would be safe, comfortable, and provided for."

Again, I blink, my mouth now hanging open. Then, my lip curls.

"You're a freak, aren't you? Expecting me to fuck you in return or something? You think I'll willingly walk into another prison, you sick fuck? Go to hell."

I hang up the phone before he can respond, my hands trembling violently. I feel sick to my stomach, and all those old memories resurface.

Doting on men and offering them pleasure at the expense of my own sanity. I was 'taken care of and provided for'. I had a roof over my head and food in my stomach at Francesca's house, too.

But that doesn't mean I wasn't dying a slow death. That I wasn't being tortured alive and driven fucking insane.

I would rather be independent and struggle than have a monster provide for me. At least when I'm alone, the only demons I'm fighting are my own.

The phone rings, startling me out of my thoughts. I jump, the phone tumbling to the ground and flying under the bed.

Cursing to myself, I get on my knees and fish it out, only to see *Unknown* flashing across the screen.

I'm tempted to smash the phone beneath my foot just so he can never reach me again. But something in my gut tells me to answer it, even if it's to curse him out again.

Just before the last ring, I flip it open and answer it.

"Listen, asshole, I don't want you call—"

"I assure you, I want nothing from you." His deep, calm voice chases away the rest of my threat.

"W-what? Why would you do this? No sane person would offer something like that with no strings attached."

"I only want you to go to a specific location and meet one of my trusted men. He's safe, and he'll set you up with a brand-new life.

I'll drop a car off for you with the keys inside, the location on the GPS, and plenty of cash for you to do with as you please. It's your choice to go, and no one will force you. No sex. No requirements outside of that. I promise you."

This is a joke. A prank. It has to be.

The sigh from the other end of the phone is almost discernible.

"I recognized you, Molly. And I can see from a mile away that you're not in a good place. I won't tell a single soul about your identity or location. I just want to help you get somewhere safe, that's all."

Fuck. Fuck, fuck, fuck, fuck. FUCK.

My heart can't take this abuse. It's only a matter of seconds before it gives out on me completely.

"Why?" I snap, my flight mode beginning to kick in. Someone *did* recognize me. And that could be catastrophic.

"It's what I do," he responds.

Not good enough of an answer.

"What's the catch?"

"You tell no one where you're going or about what my friend will do for you. Nothing else. Just your silence."

"And if I don't?"

"We will disappear without a trace before anyone could find us, and never be at your disposal again."

"At my disposal?" I repeat dumbly.

"You will come to learn that I am a valuable friend, should you ever need me again."

He speaks with a poise and confidence unlike anything I've heard before. It's almost as intimidating as it is comforting. An odd combination, and one that I feel is deadly.

I would be incredibly stupid to entertain this. Meeting with a complete stranger who is making an offer that seems far too good to be true. Especially when I've been recognized. This could be a trap. A ploy to use me for something nefarious.

No—*worse*. He could be connected to Francesca and try to bring me back to that house.

"Who do you work for?"

"I'm my own boss."

"Did anyone hire you?"

"No, Molly. I do the hiring."

Why do I believe him? No one in their right mind would consider something like this.

But my mind hasn't been right for over five years now. And at this point, what do I have to lose?

My life?

What life?

"You will have a new identity, a home, a job, a whole new life. There are very few people who deserve this more than you."

It's like he can sense I'm on the edge of a cliff and just needed one final push.

"Okay," I rush out, almost as if my mouth is racing the rational part of my brain. "But the second I feel something is off, I'm running."

Another whisper of a sigh. This one sounded relieved.

"Of course. I'll text you further directions. You won't regret this, Molly."

The line goes dead, and slowly, I pull my phone away from my ear and stare at the screen blankly.

My mind isn't racing. I'm only plagued with a single thought.

What the *fuck* am I getting myself into?

chapter twelve

MOLLY

PRESENT
2022

Layla is extremely athletic, and I have no fucking idea who she inherited that from.

Maybe our mother was, too, before she got into drugs. I doubt Dad lifted anything heavier than a vodka bottle in his years, though.

Regardless, my little sister is the star player on her soccer team, and she just scored her third goal.

I jump out of my seat and clap like there's a hornet in my face, but I refrain from cheering and screaming like I want to. I'd rather her parents think I'm an enthusiastic family member for another kid than wonder why there's a random stranger yelling their daughter's name.

"GO EMMA!" her mother, Margot, screams through the palms cupped around her mouth. Her husband and Layla's father, Colin, is right beside her, cheering with the same enthusiasm.

I'm so grateful they kept the name I gave her. It's what I would've named my own daughter, had I ever had one.

I knew that if I were going to keep Layla truly protected, then I couldn't be carrying around a missing child *as* a missing child and blatantly calling her by the name being broadcasted across the news. While I tried to avoid the public at all costs, there were times it was inevitable. And I knew that eventually, Layla was going to grow up and learn her name, and I couldn't risk her knowing who she was. It was necessary for her safety. And now, it's essential for her to continue to live a safe, happy life.

Layla's long blonde ponytail swishes behind her as she does the cutest little happy dance, her teammates running to cheer with her. My eyes grow misty, pride beaming from my chest so intensely I can hardly breathe around it.

It's impossible for me to know who she is deep down inside, but I'm confident she's the best fifteen-year-old to ever exist. Funny, smart, and popular. And from what I've seen, she's so fucking kind.

Which is the only thing that truly matters to me. That, and her being provided for and loved the way she deserves to be.

But if the couple down the row from me is any indication, she has exactly that. Their expressions resemble mine. Pride, joy, and so much love, it hurts.

Or maybe it just hurts because she doesn't know my love anymore, and I only had hers for five years of her life.

The game ends an hour later, and to no one's surprise, Layla's team wins, 4-0. The girls are assembled in a huge group, all cheering and screaming their delight.

And when her parents make their way to the group and embrace Layla in an enthusiastic hug, their mouths forming the words *I love you* and *I'm proud of you,* I turn and leave.

Tears sting at my eyes as they often do after her games. Whether it's because she won, and I can't be the one to celebrate her, or because they lost, and I'm unable to console her.

Regardless, I'm so happy for her. Because even though it's not my arms that are wrapped around her, the embrace she's in is no less loving.

This is literally the worst thing to ever happen to me, particularly in the middle of a goddamn Target.

"Marie, this is my mom, Winifred," Cage introduces us, a shit-eating grin tilting his lips. I'd love nothing more than to smack it off, but I'm currently paralyzed.

I know my eyes are the size of golf balls, and if the equally mischievous smile on his mother's face is any indication, it hasn't gone unnoticed.

She can't be much taller than five feet, peering up at me with hazel eyes. Her short white hair curls artfully around her nape and over her forehead, perfectly styled. Bright red lipstick paints her smiling lips, and she wears bedazzled black jeans and a leopard-print blouse.

"It's so nice to meet you," I squeak, holding out a slick palm for her to shake. She scoffs and bats it away before pulling me into the warmest hug I've ever experienced.

My throat tightens, but I choose to believe it's because I'm so relieved that she doesn't have to touch my sweaty hand. When I pull away, I meet Cage's gaze, only for my eyes to gravitate toward the box of condoms directly behind him.

Jesus fucking Christ.

I'm never going to recover from this.

After Layla's game, I got a call from Legion informing me that I'd be receiving another drop tonight.

For the past month, Cage has been delivering bodies three to four times a week, and each and every time, he finds a new way to end up in my bed.

Aside from the incident in the barn, I started making him use condoms. And due to his insatiable sex drive, we ran through an entire fifty-count box already.

I've tried to convince myself this past month has been some strange, lucid dream, yet the bruises on my hips and ass have made it impossible to deny.

And each night, after he'd leave, I tried telling myself to keep it strictly professional from there on out, but the twinge in my heart let me know my body heavily disagreed.

So, like any responsible thirty-four-year-old woman, I'm buying more condoms.

Just in case.

An otherwise safe endeavor. Until a presence sidled up next to me, a delicious scent invading my senses before a familiar hand pointed at a specific brand.

"I'd need these."

My wide eyes slowly processed the glaring XL on the box, then Cage's wide grin right in front of me.

Before I could utter a word, a sweet face had popped up on the other side of him, scolding him for trying to *'woo a lady in such an egregious manner.'*

"I didn't know Cage had a new lady friend!" she exclaims warmly, pulling away only to capture my cheeks between her soft hands. "Oh, the beauty of you! Your eyes are quite sexy, you know that? And that bite mark, dear Lord, it must have come from a horrible person. But, dare I say, it makes you look very edgy, my dear."

My mouth drops.

Cage sighs.

"She's going through a phase of calling women sexy. Yesterday, she told me she wanted to start wearing leather pants again," Cage explains. Despite his dry tone, his eyes glimmer with amusement.

Winifred releases me to shoot her son a disgruntled look. "That's how I seduced your father, ya know. I was wearing these skintight leather pants and a bright red halter top." She returns her stare to mine, excitement glittering in her eyes. "The girls never looked better, let me tell ya. His father took one look and had me bent over—"

"Ma," Cage intervenes sternly.

She rolls her eyes and then winks at me, a devious grin curling her red lips. "Don't worry, sweetie, I'll finish the story another time. He gets *sensitive* when I talk about my sex life in front of him."

A valid reaction, only I don't voice that. Instead, I return her smile, albeit nervously.

"Yeah, I'd, uh, love to hear it," I mumble.

"Great!" she shouts, startling a customer at the end of the aisle. I bite back a grin when the young blonde woman gives us a dumbstruck expression. Admittedly, it's hilarious, and a laugh bursts free.

Winifred doesn't even notice.

"Come over for dinner tomorrow night, and I'll tell you all the stories. I used to be a groupie back in the day. And let me just say that wannabe rock stars are better in the sack than successful ones. Once they get rich, they feel like they don't have anyone to impress." She waves her hand airily.

"Ma—"

"Anyway, can you make it? I make the best peach cobbler."

Her stare is full of so much hope, it's literally impossible to say no. I flick a glance at Cage, finding a dark and almost taunting expression. He wants me to answer, which only sends my heart rate escalating to dangerous levels.

He's obviously not feeling inclined to give me an out, and I'm unsure if it's because he's enjoying watching me struggle or because he actually wants me to come.

Either way, he's a dick.

"Y-yeah, of course. I don't have plans."

"Great!" she bellows a second time and, once again, scares the same young girl, who has since wandered closer. She jumps, drops a box as a result, and scurries to pick it up, her cheeks now bright red.

Then, the frazzled customer tosses Winifred a bewildered glance, frantically tucking flyaway blonde strands behind her ear, and hurries off before she suffers from a heart attack at an age far too young.

"Cage would love to come pick you up," she volunteers, not even bothering to check with him first. She turns to him. "Bring her over at six. And pick us up some of that good shit I like."

My brows jump.

Cage rolls his eyes. "She's referring to wine," he clarifies dryly.

Winifred refocuses on me. "And, for the love of God, wear something comfortable. We'll be sitting on a couch drinking and trash-talking my wonderful son, so please don't feel the need to impress me with a silly dress. I guarantee the ones in my closet are sexier anyway," she directs. She goes to turn away but then pivots back around. "Oh, and don't let him talk ya out of using condoms. Raising kids is so 1950s. Here, if he's anything like his father, then these should work."

I laugh when she snatches the size small condoms from the shelf and chucks them into my cart without a backward glance, then bids me farewell.

Cage's face morphs from shock to being visibly offended. "Oh, she's got jokes."

Winifred's answering cackle can be heard across several aisles, and I'm almost positive that wherever the young blonde woman is in the store, it managed to scare her again.

chapter thirteen

CAGE

NINE YEARS AGO
2013

"I WANT TO RETURN this piece-of-shit TV," the old woman snaps, her gray-and-blonde hair frazzled as she slams the receipt down on the counter.

"What was wrong with it?" my employee, Silas, asks, keeping his tone kind despite the woman's bad attitude since she first stormed in. She's short, clearly a smoker, and has her chest puffed like she's tough shit. Her bones are twigs, but whatever gets her out of bed, I guess.

"It wouldn't turn on!" she exclaims, slamming wrinkled hands on the counter. "What kind of idiot sells a TV that don't turn on?"

Silas's eye twitches, and I snicker beneath my breath.

"I kept pressing the damn clicker, and nothin'!"

"Did you make sure it was plugged in?"

The woman looks at Silas like he speaks an alien language, which seems only to enrage her further.

"Plugged into what?" she yells, her voice rising. "You know what, it don't matter. Give me my money back, you piece of shit." She tosses her receipt at Silas's chest.

It's almost impossible to contain my smile, considering I know the exact question about to come out of his mouth.

"Sure, ma'am. Where's the TV?"

Again, she stares at him like she doesn't understand.

"At my house! You think a little old lady like me can carry that in here myself? You people can't go pick it up?"

Silas is now the one staring, completely dumbfounded. I drop my head to hide my quiet laugh.

"Uh, no, ma'am. If you want to return an item, then you need to bring it in. We don't go to people's houses to retrieve it."

The lady's mouth flops for a moment, and then she proceeds to go off on a tangent. The words *'you people'* and *'pieces of shit'* are said so much, I'm ready to send her to an early grave and inscribe the words on her goddamn tombstone.

Eventually, I step in and send her off on her merry way, promising a return when she brings back the actual fucking TV. She didn't argue much. Most don't when they crack their necks simply to look up at me.

Which makes my job a fuck of a lot easier considering my regular customers aren't wanting to buy TVs. And while I've worked with quite a few grandmas, they certainly weren't harmless.

"Why are felons so much easier to deal with?" Silas grumbles, casting a dirty look at the door the old woman just exited out of.

I raise a brow. "Why do you think I created this business?"

Silas cocks his own brow mockingly. "Because you're a smart motherfucker who learned how to do something ninety-nine percent of the population can't do?"

"Ninety-nine percent is a bit of a stretch," I respond dryly. But it's not far off.

I was twelve years old when my older sister, Olivia, paid some asshole for a fake ID. I remember her being so excited, her blue eyes sparkling as she talked about getting into her first bar.

She was sixteen years old and deep in her rebellious phase.

That weekend, Olivia got dressed up with her best friend, Kelly, and they snuck out after our mom went to bed. That was the last time I saw her, and I remember vividly calling her an idiot before she climbed out of her window and ran off into the night.

The story of what happened afterward was told through the mouth of her killer during his trial.

According to Officer James Gill, he was called to the club Olivia and Kelly tried getting into. The bouncer took one look and could see their IDs were poorly made. So, to teach them a lesson, he called the police.

Officer Gill arrived at the club ten minutes later and herded them into the back seat of his cruiser. Except, he never took them to the station.

Instead, he drove them to his house that was settled by the mountains on the outskirts of town. There, he proceeded to rape and torture them for two days until he ultimately shot them both in the back of the head.

For two years, we didn't know what happened to them. Until Officer Gill kidnapped another girl, and unlike my sister and her friend, she escaped and lived to tell the police force what an evil man they had working for them.

After that, they searched his house and found Olivia, Kelly, and seven other girls buried on his property.

All I could think was that if my sister and her friend had never gotten shitty IDs, James Gill would've never entered their lives. Would've never put them in the back of his car and senselessly murdered them.

In my fourteen-year-old stupid-ass brain, I thought I was avenging my sister by learning how to make legitimate fake IDs for young women. It didn't take long before I realized I was only allowing them to enter an environment full of equally evil men. They weren't any safer and had my sister gotten in the bar that night, there's no guarantee a different man wouldn't have committed the same atrocious deed.

So, for a while, I had a skill that I didn't know how to utilize.

Until one day, a kid a few years older, David, came to me and asked if I could do more than just make him a new ID. He wanted a new life.

His dad was a general in the Marine Corps and highly abusive. David felt his life was in danger every time he went home and was convinced that if he just simply ran away, his father would find him. I guess his old man had threatened as much.

It took me two weeks to figure out how to get him a new social security card and birth certificate. I even managed to get him a job on a fishing boat.

It sparked a passion I didn't know I had. Turns out, making people disappear would be how I'd save them.

I turned eighteen and started my own business, *Black Portal,* an electronic store that sells TVs. But that was only my front. I sold my actual services by word of mouth in the beginning. Eventually, I got Legion's attention from one of my clients who knew him, and he liked what I could do and sent more clients my way. He helps bring me business; in return, I help him with favors.

My only rule—I don't help rapists or pedophiles, which isn't an issue since Legion makes those types disappear in a more permanent way. Murderers, I take case-by-case. I've helped bad guys get away, but they weren't lacking the moral compass I require if they want my help. There is such a thing as a gray area, mainly when it comes to murder.

"Jesus, is that who I think it is?" Silas whispers, his question saturated in disbelief.

My heart stops beating the second I lay eyes on her.

Molly fucking Devereaux is heading toward the counter, her eyes darting in every direction. Her shoulders are curved inward, and she's picking at her nails anxiously. Dark brown curls are deliberately arranged around her face, but those sad, green eyes and the scar on the apple of her cheek... it's a dead giveaway.

She was plastered all over the news when she went missing. And then her baby sister, Layla, eight months later. Most assume their father took Layla and ran, but neither has been seen since. Both girls with strange disappearances, which still haven't been solved to this day.

It's been almost six years since she disappeared. Now, here she is, in the flesh. And she looks no less sad than she did in her missing person poster.

"I got this one handled." I jerk my chin at Silas, signaling for him to leave us alone. Without a word, he disappears in the back.

"They say that people who have eyes like yours are destined for a tragic death."

There's a slight pause to her gait, but she pushes forward until she's a foot away, only a counter between us.

"Sanpaku eyes," I clarify. "When you have a gap below your irises."

"Do you greet all your guests by telling them they're going to go out in a ball of flames?"

"That's typically why they come to find me. I'm the one who saves them from the fire."

She hums, distracting me from counting the freckles on her nose. I only got to fifteen, but I don't mind restarting.

"I'm just here for a TV," she lies.

My answering grin is involuntary. "Sure, what kind?" I question.

"Uh—" She glances around and then points to a fifty-inch flat screen. And if I had to guess, far out of her price range. "That one."

"That'll be five hundred dollars."

Her wide eyes fly to mine. "Jesus," she mumbles. "That's literally so unnecessary."

I point toward our cheapest TV. It's a small box from a decade ago, but it has been refurbished.

"Fifty bucks for that one."

Her nose wrinkles in distaste. "That doesn't look worth more than a dollar."

"It's an antique."

"It looks better suited to host a bonfire," she retorts without hesitation.

I'm full-on smiling like a fucking fool.

"It probably is, but be careful, my employee might hear you. That's his pride and joy."

She raises a brow. "My condolences to his wounded ego."

Damn. I think I love her.

She clears her throat, realizing we've been staring at each other with stupid grins on our faces.

"So, uh, do you take payment plans for putting out fires?"

I lean my arms on the counter, now looking up at her from beneath my brows. I can feel how wicked it is, but I'm unable to hide it.

"First, tell me your name. Mine is Cage Everhart."

She narrows her eyes, seemingly suspicious.

"You're telling me you don't know who I am? Legion didn't tell you I was coming?"

I grin, appreciating her observation.

"Legion actually didn't warn me, the fucker. But while I do recognize you, I wanted to be careful in case you go by something else."

She hums, then answers, "Molly. You can call me Molly."

I hold out a hand for her to shake, which she grabs timidly. The second her skin touches mine, it feels like tiny electrical currents zapping between our palms.

"Nice to meet you, Molly," I rasp.

If I had to hold her hand forever, it wouldn't be long enough. However, she releases me and pulls out a black card from the back pocket of her dark blue jeans, appearing unsure. "Legion?"

She says it like it's a question, though the gold letters say just that.

I've seen this card a handful of times. And every time, the person handing it over is someone who desperately needs an escape.

It also means Legion is completely covering their fee. And my prices are steep.

"Do you know where you want to go?" I ask, brushing my thumb over the foil letters. Usually, I keep the card, but I slide it back to her for reasons I can't explain. Hesitantly, she grabs it and tucks it in her jeans again.

"Alaska." The answer seems to burst from her throat, as if it's been imprisoned behind her teeth.

I raise a brow in surprise. Most people try to go to the beach, where it's warm and makes them feel like they've escaped to a tropical island. I *could* send people to places like that, but most can't afford that hefty fee.

Ultimately, they go where I send them, though I do try to find somewhere they're happy with. Especially if they deserve that peace.

"You like the cold?"

She shrugs, and it seems as if she's battling with her next words.

"If I'm out in the wilderness, just me and the wolves, no one will find me. No one will recognize me. I've disappeared once. This time, I want it to be for good."

My tongue forms the words to ask what happened to her that day. Who was chasing her? Did they put that haunted look in her eyes? How did she escape? And what is driving her to stay hidden from the world?

"It's going to take my team a good twenty-four hours to obtain everything," I tell her.

Her fingers tap on the counter, and she chews on her lip nervously.

"Does this happen to come with accommodations before I leave?" she questions, her cheeks beginning to flush red with embarrassment. "I, uhm, I don't really have anywhere to go while I wait."

Legion will cover all her expenses, including food and necessities. If she has that black card, she might as well have his credit card.

But I don't tell her that part. Not yet, at least.

"Sure," I say. "We'll help get you set up in a hotel. Legion will cover you."

Her shoulders fall in relief, but mine tighten.

It's a feeling I can't name. One that probably has some fucking obscure word to describe it. But knowing this may be the last time I see her before she leaves doesn't settle right with me. In fact, it makes me downright desperate to ensure it's not my last moment with her.

Not because of who she is and what happened to her. But because, for some indescribable reason, she feels like mine.

"Give me a second to get some things sorted. Stay put, yeah?"

"Yeah," she croaks, casting another glance around.

She's uncomfortable, and I decide immediately that I really fucking hate that.

It's not easy pulling my gaze away from her, but I force myself to turn and head into the back. Silas is standing in front of a stack of boxed TVs, a clipboard in his hand as he sorts through inventory.

"Go out front and keep an eye on her? Make sure she's not recognized. I'll only be a minute."

"You got it," he chirps, before setting down his clipboard and heading out to the front.

I wait a few minutes, ensuring he isn't around, then I pull out my phone and get to work. Within a minute, I'm calling the first hotel.

"Thank you for calling the *Milton Hotels*. How may I help you?" a woman greets, her voice high-pitched.

"I'd like to book every available room for the night."

There's a pause. "I-I'm sorry, you said *all* available rooms?"

"Yes, please. Every single room. Until you're fully booked and don't have a single fucking one to spare."

"Uhm, okay. Sure."

Once that's done, I proceed to call every hotel within a thirty-mile radius and book them out, too.

chapter fourteen

MOLLY

NINE YEARS AGO
2013

"Do you have a computer I can use to find a hotel?" I ask, tapping my fingers against the counter nervously. Cage just returned from the back, and anxiety is gnawing at my stomach.

This entire situation is so far out of my depth, and I feel a little sick if I analyze it too deeply.

So easily, I could be walking into another wolf's den. I'm not sure if escaping human trafficking has made me cautious or reckless at this point. Everything I do feels like my life is on the line, and I'm not sure if I'll live long enough to know peace.

"Silas will book the room for you and get it taken care of," Cage offers.

His employee doesn't waste another second and pulls out his phone, googling nearby hotels.

"Right. Thanks," I mumble.

"Do you need anything in the meantime? Water? Food?"

I blink. Food has been more of a luxury than a necessity, and I've gotten good at ignoring the hunger pangs. For as long as I can remember, it's always been a fight to fuel my body. And I don't know if I've ever been offered food and water in all my twenty-five years of life.

"Uh, I guess water would be nice," I say, my cheeks burning.

"Sure, thanks," Silas mutters on the phone before hanging up, his brow pinched. "That's the second hotel I've called that is completely booked."

Cage glances at him. "Keep trying. I'm sure there's at least one that has an available room." Then, his stare returns to mine. "It's about dinnertime for us anyway. We're open for another hour, and I suppose it's not smart to take you out in public, so I can order a pizza if you'd like?"

My lips part, but I have no words. I'm not sure why, but it's embarrassing that he wants to feed me. I know I'm malnourished—but I guess I don't like that it's so obvious.

However, I'm too hungry to turn it down.

"Sure. That'd be nice. Thank you."

"What toppings do you like on your pizza?"

I flush hotter and avoid eye contact, deciding to settle my gaze on my chipped nails. "I've never had pizza before, so I don't really know. I guess just cheese is fine."

When I do find the courage to flick a glance in his direction, I'm almost impressed by how easily he schools his expression. He doesn't gape at me like I'd expected. Instead, a sly grin curls his lips.

"Then let me be the one to introduce you to the best thing you'll ever eat in your life. I'll get a supreme, maybe a Hawaiian if you're the type to like pineapple on your pizza—huge debate in the world, by the way—and of course, a plain cheese and a pepperoni just in case."

My eyes nearly pop out of my skull as he goes on. "Oh my God, no. That is so much food! You really don't have to do th—"

He leans heavily on the counter across from me, cutting off whatever the hell I was going to say. He peers up at me with a challenging expression, but what has me tongue-tied is the raw animalistic energy that radiates from him. I don't know if he's even aware of it, yet it sets me on fucking fire anyway.

"I know I don't have to. But I like to eat," he drawls lazily.

My chest tightens, and a swarm of butterflies flutter in the pit of my stomach. It doesn't sound like he's declaring his affection for consuming *food* at this moment.

It feels as if a sharp, pointed claw is poised against the inside of my throat, and it slowly drags down my chest, into my stomach, and between my thighs, leaving a hot trail in its wake.

I'm tempted to make some corny joke about being out of practice with eating, though I know how to swallow. Except I don't have the confidence to say something like that. Nor am I sure if I'd even want to.

Sex isn't something I'm interested in. Not after going through everything that I have. In fact, I'm perfectly content if I never have to see another penis for the rest of my life.

Yet, the way Cage stares up at me now—I wonder if that's really true.

I hadn't considered what sex would be like if I *chose* it, and if it's something that would feel good.

"Goddamn it!" Silas shouts, startling me damn near out of my skin. Cage cranes his head over his shoulder, glaring at his employee.

"Sorry," he mutters. "I've called every fucking hotel nearby, and all of them are booked. How is that even possible?"

My heart drops, and immediately, my thoughts begin to spiral. I have Legion's car and could probably sleep in it for the night. It's not safe, but if I find a parking lot with other cars, maybe no one will notice.

"Th-that's okay. I can find somewhere else to st—"

"Absolutely not," Cage interrupts, straightening his spine. "I have a spare bedroom. You can stay with me tonight."

My mouth flops for a few moments before I raise my hands, finally scrounging up the voice to protest. "N-no. That's so not necessary. I'll find—"

"If you're even considering sleeping somewhere outside, I'm going to have to stop you there. That's too dangerous."

A crease forms between my brows. "And staying with a complete stranger isn't?"

His features relax slightly, and he offers a soft grin.

"Call Legion. He'll put guards outside my house. The second you scream for help, they'll come running, and I'll have a bullet through my brain before I can blink."

"A bullet? That... that also seems unnecessary."

He cocks a brow. "Is it?"

An image of my father being ripped apart by pigs flashes through my brain, and I relent, "I guess not."

"For what it's worth, I would never hurt you. I promise not to lay a finger on you." There's a pause, and I hear the unspoken words he won't give voice to.

Unless you ask me to.

A large part of me is glad he didn't say it. But another part of me is a little disappointed. Maybe because I don't know that I'll ever gather the courage to say that I *do* want him to.

He nods toward me. "Call Legion."

The black flip phone burns in my back pocket, and I'm tempted to pull it out and do just that. But what if Legion is no better of a man than Cage? If he led me to someone willing to hurt me, then I doubt he's an upstanding guy, either.

And I'd rather fight one man in a place where I have access to a knife than a man when I'm alone in a car.

Do I feel safe with Cage? No. But not because I think he'll hurt me.

Only that it'll hurt when I need to leave.

I don't know why I feel safe with him, just that I do. And if there's one thing I've gotten really good at over the years, it's trusting my gut.

"It's fine," I force out. "I'll take your word for it."

"How old are you?" I ask, though my voice is breathless with awe as my stare bounces around his home.

"Twenty-seven," he answers instantly.

I've never seen a twenty-seven-year-old own a house like this. It's *beautiful*.

The interior is a combination of black stone, veneer wooden panels, and cream walls. Plant life is scattered throughout the open floor plan, complementing the earthy-toned furniture.

The living room is sunken in from the kitchen, two rounded steps leading down to where a massive, circular black couch sits in front of a fireplace, a huge TV mounted above it.

To my left is a sleek kitchen with a huge island in the middle. There, Cage lays the cardboard stack of pizza boxes, left over from a few hours ago. The supreme was my favorite, and I found the cheese too boring. To Silas's dismay, I didn't mind the pineapple on the pizza, though it wouldn't be something I'd order for myself.

"You can have more if you're still hungry," Cage offers, nodding toward the food.

"I'm full," I protest. I've never eaten so much in my life, even if it was only four slices.

I grew up eating ketchup sandwiches on stale bread and soup when I was with Francesca. Greasy, fried foods were a luxury I never knew.

His stare slides down my form slowly before returning to mine. By the time he's finished, I'm on fire and shifting on my feet, my thighs clenching from the pulse between them.

"You'll be hungry again soon enough."

I don't know what that means. But the way his voice roughened has me shifting once again.

"We'll see," I retort, feeling as if I just issued a challenge. His darkening eyes seem to confirm that.

I almost expect him to shatter the pretense that this is an innocent sleepover and strip me down where I stand. Instead, he turns away and gestures for me to follow him.

I can't decipher why I feel disappointed by that, just that I do.

"The guest bedroom is this way," he calls. It takes an extra second to unglue my feet from the wooden floor and follow him. "Do you need to shower?"

That question nearly stops me in my tracks again. I had a shower at the motel I stayed in last night, but the water pressure was comparable to a yard sprinkler, the drain was clogged, and the tub held more rust and grime than soap.

A shower in a place like this just might be the closest to heaven I'll ever get.

"Y-yeah, if you don't mind," I manage. However, the second the words leave my mouth, I wonder if I'm being incredibly stupid. Or rather, stupid-*er*. Showering in a stranger's home, naked and vulnerable. Not that I'm much more protected with a scrappy t-shirt and torn jeans, but at least I'd die with a bit of dignity.

"I have a towel and washcloth for you. A spare toothbrush, too, if you need it. Even razors."

I chew my bottom lip, feeling a small burst of excitement. Admittedly, it's been a long time since I've had the luxury of shaving my legs.

"All of it," I rush out, then instantly flush with embarrassment over my clear desperation for a decent shower. Clearing my throat, I tack on, "Please."

I can't see his face, but I know he's grinning.

He leads me into a spacious hallway, where an ornate gothic stone bench is placed on the left side, an array of different plants covering it, and beautiful artwork surrounding it. We veer off to the left and enter through double doors that open into a massive bedroom.

"This is the guest bedroom?" I ask incredulously, taking in the biggest bed I've ever seen covered in soft black sheets, the crackling fireplace on the opposite wall, and the white ceiling with beautiful black wooden beams lining across it.

"One of them, yeah."

"I can't imagine what the master looks like then," I mumble, a funny look passing over my face.

He turns, a devilish look on his face as he asks, "Would you like to see it?"

"Nope. Bigger isn't always better," I quip, noting the open door to my left where I can see a black stone vanity. I head toward it without waiting for his response, and his burning stare doesn't abate as it follows me. "I assume the bathroom is already stocked with what I need?"

"Sure is," he drawls deeply.

My stomach flutters as I hurry into the bathroom, too much of a chicken to spare him a glance. By the time I get the door shut and lean heavily against it, my heart is pounding.

He'll be waiting for me to finish, and what comes after will be something I've never done before.

I'm going to fuck him.

And for the first time, it'll be my choice.

I'm so fucking nervous, but it doesn't feel... bad. In fact, it's exhilarating. It's a foreign emotion, but I can understand why people get addicted to it.

Because at this moment, I've never felt more alive.

chapter fifteen

CAGE

PRESENT
2022

WHEN I WAS A kid, my grandma once convinced me that my mother came out of the womb talking.

I'm *still* convinced of it.

"So, I told her, 'Ma'am, if you're going to keep talkin' all that shit, at least carry some toilet paper with you to wipe your damn mouth.'"

Molly cups a hand over her smiling lips, green eyes glittering with mirth as she shakes her head at my mom.

She used to embarrass the absolute shit out of me and Olivia. But once we lost my sister, I found a new appreciation for her eccentric personality. She's all I have in this world, and despite her utter heartbreak over her daughter's death, she always showed up for me. Never let me down, despite how hard the world tried to kick her to the ground.

"I don't like bullies. What do you kids call 'em these days? Karens? Well, she was one of them. Except I just called her what she really is, which is a defective sperm that grew too much of a mouth instead of a brain."

"You're such a poet, Ma," I comment dryly.

The tiger lilies I had just bought Mom are arranged in the crystal vase she's had for decades at the center of the dinner table, our empty plates and wineglasses in front of us.

I pull out my pack of nicotine gum and shove one in my mouth. I'm tempted to eat the whole sleeve of them now that we've finished dinner. Mom already served the peach cobbler, which I skipped. I'm not much of a sweets person.

Unless, of course, it's Molly's pussy.

"Am I? Next time, I'll charge ya just to listen to me speak then," she retorts. "All this time, and I coulda been getting rich just from yelling at you."

I chuckle, glancing at Molly and finding her biting back a smile. One of these days, I'll teach her how to set them free.

"Have some more to drink," Mom encourages, pouring more red wine into Molly's glass. "With as stiff as you are, I fear my son will be marrying a wooden puppet. He'll be picking splinters out of his—"

"Jesus fucking Christ," I groan. "Quit talking."

"I'll make sure to buy him a magnifying glass then," Molly says, one corner of her lips curled upward.

"For the splinters or his penis?"

"*Ma.*"

A laugh bursts from Molly's throat, and instantly, I forgive my mother for being so crass. I'm used to her making jokes at my expense, but I'm confident Molly has never met anyone like my mother, and her personality definitely isn't a one-size-fits-all. There's been a few girlfriends in the past that she's scared off, which instantly told me they weren't worth it anyway.

"I'm not gonna scare ya off, am I?" Mom asks her, as if reading my mind.

She shakes her head. "I don't scare that easily. Not anymore, at least."

"See? She's tough," Mom tells me, then focuses on Molly, a sly grin on her face. She's going to say something terrible, except I don't have time to stop her. "How viable is your uterus? Eggs haven't shriveled yet, right? I've been waiting for grandkids."

"I'm sorry about her," I apologize, leading Molly into my childhood room. "Believe it or not, she doesn't ask about every woman's uterus that I've brought around."

She gives me a guarded look. "How many women have you brought around?"

My expression is serious as I say, "Two. And they were hopeless attempts at trying to make myself feel what I felt with you."

She turns away, choosing not to answer.

"My mom really likes you," I tell her, refusing to let her run away, even if it's in her own mind.

"She hardly knows me," Molly argues softly, running her fingers over a high school soccer trophy.

"She knows all that she needs to," I say, shrugging a shoulder.

She raises a brow. "What have you told her?"

I grin. "Only the important parts. That you're incredibly strong, funny, and the most amazing woman I've ever met. I think she can see that already."

"What if she's wrong? We're not even dating."

My muscles tighten, and my teeth clench. I'm overcome with the urge to show her just how wrong she is. She's mine, as explicitly as the heart in my chest.

I'm advancing on her before she can slide her fingers across another trophy. Her breath halts as I crowd into her, my chest molding against her back. She shivers as I lean in closely, feathering my lips across the shell of her ear.

Those little tremors are not nearly enough.

I want her to fucking convulse like she's being possessed, and it'll be my cock inside her while she does.

"You think I need an anniversary date to put my baby inside you?"

I don't recognize my own voice anymore, but I do find that little gasp familiar.

"You wouldn't," she breathes. "We hardly know each other."

"No," I agree. "Not yet, at least." I place a kiss below her ear. "But I would. I absolutely—" Kiss. "—fucking—" Kiss. "—would."

She whips around, those fiery eyes pinned to mine as she snaps, "I wouldn't let you. What if I find you to be absolutely insufferable? You could leave food crusted on your dishes instead of rinsing them off. Or have dirty clothes all over the floor and soggy towels on the bed." She pauses and glances nervously to the side. "You could find my nightmares intolerable."

"You don't think I have them?" I question, enjoying the feeling of her heart beating against my chest. "I've suffered in life, too, baby. Just in different ways."

"You have nightmares?" she questions curiously.

In response, I grab her hand and pull her after me.

"Where...?

She trails off as I lead her out of my old room, down the hall, and to the last door on the right.

She doesn't speak as she takes in the pale yellow walls, blue-and-yellow duvet, and the pictures pinned to the corkboard hanging above her white desk. Pictures of a blonde-haired girl sticking her tongue out next to friends or holding up the peace sign and pursing her lips.

She was beautiful.

"Her name was Olivia. She was murdered when she was sixteen, and I was twelve. It ultimately led me to get into the business I'm in. She and her friend were caught trying to get into a nightclub with a fake ID. Her killer was a cop who came to pick them up, and she never came home."

"I'm sorry," Molly whispers, slowly walking up to the photos and studying them closely. "Not many people come home."

"You did, though, didn't you?"

Slowly, she turns her head just enough to peer at me over her shoulder.

"If anyone deserved to be the one to escape, it would've been her." She turns away, but not before I see the sadness polluting her eyes. "Turns out, I wasn't important enough to deserve it. I thought Layla needed me, but I think I only delayed her happiness. My father was being investigated, and eventually, CPS would've found him unfit anyway. I was convinced she'd just go to another unfit home, but what if she didn't? What if she found a good home, rather than me taking her away to live four miserable years with me? No stability. Being hungry all the time—" Her voice cracks, and she cuts herself off abruptly.

"You're wrong, ya know," I tell her, fire building in my chest. "Or, at least, there's a good chance you are. She would've gone into the system, and there's no guarantee she would've ended up with a good family. She could've gone from one abuser to the next."

Molly nods, the movement choppy, but she doesn't appear convinced.

I'm furious that she could think so little of herself. Even more furious at the people who made her feel as though she's not a goddamn goddess walking this earth that we don't deserve.

"You are the most important person I've ever met, Molly," I whisper. "And while I will always be devastated that my sister didn't survive, I'm so fucking happy that you did."

Though her back is facing me, I hear a soft sniffle. She doesn't respond. Instead, she stares at Olivia, that smile on her face forever frozen in time.

"For years, I couldn't step foot in this room. Anytime I saw those pictures with her smiling face, it would slowly morph into a dramatic frown, her mouth opening on a wail. It looked fucking demonic, and I had all but convinced myself that was the real expression frozen on her face when she died. Her cries of terror outlived her heartbeat."

"Do you want to talk about her?" Molly asks quietly, voice clogged with tears. "I'd like to get to know her."

My chest tightens, and I can't tell if I want to wrap her in my arms because she cares, or because I need something to hold on to while I tell her about my sister.

"She loved 80s music. 'Sunglasses at Night' by Corey Hart was her favorite song, and she insisted on constantly wearing these neon pink sunglasses for three months after she heard it for the first time. Mom thought she was the cutest thing, and I made it a point to tell her how ridiculous she looked."

Molly's head swivels to find the picture of Olivia wearing them, a bright smile pasted on her face as she sits beside me in our mom's car, my face slackened in a dry, unamused expression. She'd just gotten her driver's license that day and, of course, blasted that Corey Hart song all the way home.

"She wore pink lipstick every day, even when she was sick. She always said the version of her without it was her evil alter ego. She hated tomatoes but put ketchup on everything, even her mashed potatoes. Which I still find very fucking gross, by the way."

"I would have to agree with that," Molly chuckles softly.

Her stare slides to a picture of Olivia sitting beside a bald little boy in a hospital bed, with birthday hats atop their heads.

"When she turned sixteen, she spent her birthday at the children's hospital in the cancer unit because she felt guilty that they may never see that age."

My heart aches, and for a moment, it feels impossible to continue.

"She never knew she wouldn't see past that age, either."

Molly turns to me, sadness swirling in her gaze.

"She sounds like she was an incredible kid," she whispers. "Amazing, really."

I nod, working to swallow past the rock in my throat.

Almost shyly, she grabs my hand and walks me over to Olivia's bed. I'm not sure what she intends, but my head is too fuzzy to ask.

With a slight smile on her face, she lies down on one side of the bed and pats the empty spot next to her. Confused, I follow suit, the both of us staring up at the ceiling silently. Right as I begin to ask her what she's doing, a burst of music fills the room.

My eyes flick to where she holds her phone up, "Sunglasses at Night" playing from the speakers.

"Mol—"

"Shh," she hushes, laying her hand over mine. "Don't be rude. Olivia might be trying to listen, too."

I can't breathe.

A fire explodes in my chest, burning a path down to our entwined hands.

I hope to God that it burns her, too.

I want the flames to melt our hands together so she can never let go.

If she wanted me to fall in love with her, she only needed to tell me. Now, she has no choice in the matter.

Though, I suppose she never really did.

Turning my head, I stare at her until she meets my eyes. "I will chase away all your nightmares until they grow wary of returning. They will fear me, my little ghost. But you never will."

chapter sixteen

MOLLY

NINE YEARS AGO
2013

I DON'T KNOW THAT I've felt so clean in my entire life. Nor has my skin ever been so smooth.

A towel is wrapped tightly around my body, and my hair tumbles over my shoulders in a mass of curls, water dripping from the ends.

Anxiety is holding every last one of my nerves hostage. I'm standing at the door, staring at it as if it's the mirror on the wall from *Snow White*, and it's going to tell me my future.

Will I like sex?

I've never had an orgasm before. Too caught up in trying to survive to even consider it. I've always avoided intimacy or anything to do with sex. After what my father did to me, and then everything that happened in Francesca's house—I never felt inclined to try.

Now, I wish I had. If I don't even know what I like, how will he?

I'm too much in my head.

Surely, he can figure it out.

Inhaling deeply, I swing open the door and find the room empty. That's both disappointing and relieving. Had he been standing there, I probably wouldn't know what to do with myself. But that means I'm going to have to seek him out now. Which sounds equally terrifying.

What the fuck am I even supposed to say to him?

Hi, excuse me, can you put your dick inside me? I'm not sure if I'll like it, but let's find out together.

I'm going to embarrass myself. I just know it.

I walk over to the bed, noticing a pile of clothing folded atop. They look like men's clothing, and when I pick up the soft black t-shirt, I'm instantly hit with a delectable scent—a mix of vetiver and sandalwood.

My eyes nearly roll, and I'm unabashed in the way I practically stuff the soft fabric up my nose.

"Smell good?"

The voice is so sudden, there's no containing the loud screech that bursts from my throat. I drop the shirt while I whip around, my towel unraveling from the quick movement. I catch it before it falls completely, then bar my arm across my breasts and hold it there, though it only manages to cover my center. With my other hand, I grip the towel against my stomach, keeping it from swaying and exposing me further.

My heart is on the verge of exploding out of my chest, and I'm too stunned to get my shit together and cover myself properly. At this moment, I hardly remember how to breathe. My lungs are functioning no better than an old, rusty engine that was left abandoned in a junkyard.

Green eyes darken, a red-hot flame burning within. They blaze a trail over my exposed flesh, unashamed by the way his stare so readily devours me. I don't miss the way it catches on the white bite marks imprinted on my skin. My hips, my thighs, my stomach...

His teeth visibly clench, rage flashing across his gaze.

"What?" The delayed question comes out as a breathless squeak.

Nostrils flaring, he takes a step toward me, and the battered muscle in my chest flies up into my throat. I lock my knees, forcing myself to stand still despite how much I want to back away.

Distinctly, I feel a bead of water drip onto the swell of my breast, which his gaze immediately tracks. The droplet slowly trails down the valley between my breasts, and the muscle in his jaw pulses, nearly tearing through his skin. His animalistic gaze snaps up to mine, his chin tipping low as he stares at me fiercely from beneath thick brows.

Heat gathers low in my stomach, sinking down between my trembling thighs. My clit pulses from that single look alone, and I know that if he were to part my legs, he'd see the evidence glistening from within.

Never in my life have I *ever* felt this way. Never has my core felt so... empty.

He's silent as he stalks toward me, but I'm positive my escalated heart rate is audible.

I shift on my feet, feeling how slick I've become. It's almost embarrassing, yet it's a reaction the men in Francesca's house would claim, but never actually accomplished. They wanted us to weep for them, but the only thing they ever made wet was our eyes.

Cage, on the other hand, easily makes my pussy weep, and he hasn't even touched me yet.

He stops an inch before me, the heat radiating from him warming my skin. Goosebumps scatter across my flesh, and a shiver tumbles down my spine. It feels as if bees are buzzing beneath the surface, their fluttering wings creating electricity and engulfing my body in it.

"Do you want me to leave?" he asks quietly.

It's a question that requires a simple answer. Yes or no. Yet, my brain turns it over as if he presented me with a complicated math equation.

The throbbing between my legs screams its answer, though my head can do nothing but focus on how I have no idea what the fuck I'm doing.

"I-I'm not very good at this," I mumble, keeping my eyes pinned to his chest. I'm not brave enough to meet his stare. It'll eat me alive, and I'm too afraid that I'll allow it to chase me away before I can let him touch me.

"Has anyone made you feel good before?"

I lick my lips, feeling like any moisture in my body has flooded south.

"No."

"Then that's all you need to do. You don't need to do anything else, except let me make you feel good."

My nod is choppy, and the butterflies in my stomach have been freed. But they're hungry, too, and they've begun to tear at my insides. Especially as his forefinger hooks beneath my chin and forces it up, until my stare snaps to his like a magnet.

"Where do you want me to kiss first?" he asks, his tone hushed, deep and rough.

Silently, I reach up and brush my fingers across my lips, drawing his attention there.

He's slow to lean in, as if to prolong the torture. But the second his lips capture mine between his, I wish he'd given me an extra moment to breathe.

The kiss is short, but primal and entirely too explosive for only a second. It's nothing like those pecks I've seen on TV, and I can't imagine they felt the pure fire that's raging between us.

He watches me for half a second before he crushes his mouth back onto mine, evoking a volcanic eruption that's melting me into a pile of ash. Yet, he holds on to all the pieces of me and gathers them against his chest until there is no me and him. Only an us.

His hand slides along my jawline and dives into my damp curls, directing the angle of my head so he can lick along the seam of my lips. And like a greedy little puppet, I eagerly open for him. He tastes the smallest of gasps on his tongue as it glides against mine, which seems only to invigorate him.

It transforms from a passionate kiss to being devoured whole, and the only thing I can do is submit. I'm a slave to him, and it's the first time I'm happy to be one.

In a moment of madness, I drop my towel altogether, the thump over my feet causing him to pull away, though his lips rest against mine.

"Where do you want me to kiss next?" he rasps.

I've never heard a voice so deep, bordering on demonic. It would make sense why I feel so possessed.

"Lower," I rasp.

He places an open-mouthed kiss on my jaw, ending it there.

"Let me hear your words," he purrs. "Do you want me to kiss these pretty tits? Or I can kiss your sweet pussy. I'll fucking feast on her if you want."

"Yes," I moan. "All of it."

He dips at the knees just enough to grab the backs of my thighs and lift me up, my feet hooking behind his back. But it's useless because, within moments, he's laying me on the bed and descending my body, wasting no time wrapping his lips around my nipple.

A shot of electricity races down my spine, and my back bows off the bed, a cry slipping past my lips.

"Cage!"

His answering growl is primal, followed by the sharp bite of his teeth. My mouth falls open on a silent scream, my body unable to properly function beneath the assault.

Every one of my nerves is hyper-fixated on the way his tongue swirls over me. Then, he switches to the other, cupping both of my breasts in his large palms as if he's feeding them into his mouth.

My fingers dive into his short strands, scraping my nails against his scalp.

His teeth gnash at my abused nipple one more time before he pulls away, taking his wet kisses lower.

My lungs tighten, refusing to pull in a single breath as he reaches my belly button. There lies a scar that's fitted perfectly around it.

Aside from the one on my face, I've always hated that one most because of how ugly and centered on my body it is.

I'm prepared to tell him to ignore it, but before I can manage a sound, he's matching his teeth to the scar and sinking them into it.

"Cage!" I screech, the burning pain encompassing my shock.

When he lifts his wicked stare to mine, I see a mix of rage and something I could only describe as possession.

"I will claim every part of you, Molly. And that includes the pieces of you those fuckers tried to take from me."

My brows pinch. "From you?" I repeat dumbly.

Deliberately, he places a kiss over the bite.

"Don't be fooled, little ghost, I will own you even after you've disappeared. You may vanish, but your soul will always be mine."

I'm not sure if it's normal for one-night stands to be so damn intense. It sounds like a proclamation of love without saying the words. Except way more... permanent.

Yet, he may as well have gathered any resolve I had left and crushed it beneath his boot. He's so intense, but there isn't an iota of me that cares right now. He feels too good, and if it continues this way, maybe he'll be right.

Though it won't stop me from becoming a ghost.

It's the only thing I know how to be.

His stare drops, and he resumes his path toward my pussy, pausing briefly to bite over the white scars on my hip and thighs. Each time, it grows more intense. By the time his hot breath fans over my center, I'm trembling.

"Cage," I whisper, feeling as if I'm on the verge of combusting. I need so much more, but I'm also not sure if I can handle what's next.

He inhales, and my eyes widen in mortification. Before I can slap him or move away, he's parting my thighs and covering my clit with his mouth. Except he doesn't lick me yet, depriving me of the sensation my body needs so desperately.

"Please," I groan impatiently.

Grinning devilishly, he delivers the smallest lick, sending a shock wave up my spine.

My back arches, and the strangest confidence washes over me.

"Please lick my pussy. I need you to make me feel good," I plead. "You promised."

"Fuck," he curses a moment before he flattens his tongue and glides it up my slit. My outcry is answered by another thorough lick, in which he groans deeply.

"Christ, baby, you taste so sweet, I don't know how I'll stop. I would gladly drown in the prettiest cunt I've ever eaten."

His words are filthy, but the way he continuously flicks his pointed tongue over my clit is entirely depraved. There's no time to prepare for the sharp sensations invading every inch of my insides. I'm overcome with pure bliss, and for several heartbeats, the only sound I can muster is a loud moan.

"Oh, ffu— Oh my God, Cage."

He doesn't relent, and within moments, I'm hurtling toward a far more powerful sensation. Pleasure, euphoria—they're too weak of words to describe the hurricane building inside of me.

"Oh, please, don't stop." Yet, that's exactly what he does. "Cage!" I shout as he pulls away, only to dive his tongue into my pussy, curling it upward.

I writhe beneath him, grinding my hips against him and hoping to God he does fucking drown. My nails scrape against his scalp, and if I could hook them beneath his flesh and force him to make me come, I'd happily show him what it means to be a puppet.

My eyes roll as I get close again, and for the second time, he pulls away.

A frustrated scream bursts from my throat, but before I can spit a threat at him, he grabs the underside of my thighs and pushes them forward until my lower back is lifted off the bed and my knees are hiked to my ears. I'm folded in half, my core less than a foot from my face.

Within seconds, his mouth is covering my pussy again, and this time, he's showing me exactly what he's doing to me. With perfect precision, he strokes my clit, my arousal and his saliva pouring down my mound and dripping onto my breasts.

Cries stream from my throat as I grip his forearms, red crescents forming in his flesh. Once more, he's driving me directly toward the edge. My thighs shake violently in his hold as he feasts on me like a starving animal driven to madness from hunger.

"Cage, I'm going to come. Please, *please*, let me come," I beg breathlessly. "Let me drown you."

A growl unleashes from his chest, vibrating against me. Dark green eyes are pinned to me as he viciously sucks on my clit, his tongue unrelenting.

My throat closes and my vision blackens a moment before I explode. The scream that unleashes is so sharp, it leaves my throat raw. Colorful fireworks detonate behind my pinched eyes, filling the blackness with a mirage of blues, pinks, greens, and purples.

I don't know how long I'm submerged beneath the storm, but distinctly, I can feel my body seizing furiously. Yet, he holds on to me with a firm grip, keeping me in place as he continues to lap at my cunt until I have nothing left to give.

After what feels like forever, I come down from an experience that could only be described as an exorcism.

"Jesus f-fucking Christ," I stutter, my voice cracking and shaken, my mouth almost feeling numb.

His gaze is fierce. "If you're asking Him to save you, then I will nail Him onto that fucking cross again. You will be my ruin, but only *I* will be your savior."

chapter seventeen

MOLLY

NINE YEARS AGO
2013

EVEN IF I HAD the brain function to respond, I wouldn't know how.

Gently, he drops my trembling legs back onto the bed, only to draw his t-shirt over his head.

Jesus fucking Christ.

I keep the words to myself this time, but a small gasp manages to slip free.

His body is sculpted better than the marble statues of gods in museums across the world. Chiseled to pure perfection, with black tattoos covering his stomach, chest, and down his arms.

The gray sweatpants he's wearing do nothing to hide his hard cock, and the moment I lay eyes on it, I immediately wish I hadn't. In this case, maybe ignorance would've been bliss.

"Cage, I don't know if I can handle it," I say hesitantly, now extremely cautious of trying to take all of him inside me. I'm unsure how I'd even fit it in my goddamn *mouth*.

"It'll fit, baby," he assures confidently, hooking his thumbs into the waistband of his sweats and sliding them down his thick thighs, and off his legs.

His cock is even more intimidating without the clothing over it, and much bigger than I thought. But, fuck, is it beautiful. Long and deliciously thick, with pulsing veins cording throughout it. He's perfectly proportioned, and even the swollen head has me aching to suck on it.

"Keep staring at me like that, and I'll give that little mouth of yours more than it can handle."

It takes effort to drag my gaze up to his, my expression twisted with apprehension. "That's not going to fit."

He grins devilishly. "It'll fit."

I give him a look that tells him just how wrong I think he is, though that only widens his smirk. He oozes confidence, and while I'm still incredibly terrified of the beast between his legs, I do feel at ease that he knows what he's doing.

"Do you want to watch me prove you wrong?" he asks lowly, his voice deepening. Reaching over to his discarded sweats, he plunges his hand into the pocket and produces a foil packet.

He brought protection.

Relief washes over me. So much so that I don't hesitate to whisper, "Yes."

I'm enthralled by the way he expertly slides the condom over his thick length, and I'm short of breath when he prowls up my body, hovering over me. My stomach tightens when he leans down and brushes the faintest of kisses over my lips, eliciting crackling static between them.

"I'll feed my cock into your pussy nice and slow, okay, baby? I'll make sure you're so fucking full, then just when you think you can't take any more—" His lip pulls up into a savage snarl. "—I'll go deeper."

That's not just a promise, but a threat.

"What if I can't take it?" I question, my tone husky with desire.

He trails his lips over my jawline and to the shell of my ear. Just before he places a soft kiss below my lobe, he murmurs darkly, "You've survived much worse."

His tone is unapologetic, indicating that he's confident in my ability to survive *him*. My stomach clenches around the anxious butterflies within.

Once more, he's lifting the underside of my thighs, hooking them over his arms as he positions the tip at my entrance. He applies just enough pressure to part my lips, but not enough to breach past my opening.

I've never been on a roller coaster, except this is precisely what I imagine it feels like when it crests over the hill right before the big drop. The anticipation is nearly as terrifying as it is thrilling.

"Cage," I breathe shakily, needing him to do something—anything—but leave me in suspense.

"Take me," he commands roughly. I shake my head, at a loss for what he needs me to do. Only then my pussy contracts and it feels like my body is suctioning him in.

"Fuuuuck, that's it," he rasps, the both of us watching the tip of his cock disappear. "So goddamn tight, *fuck,* Molly."

"I— What—"

"It's a natural reaction, baby. Most men just aren't patient enough to wait for a woman's pussy to invite him in," he explains tightly.

I didn't know that was possible, but he's pushing his hips deeper, and I no longer care. I'm too focused on learning how to breathe again, yet it seems like a futile effort. Just as he promised, he feeds his cock into me until I'm on the verge of bursting.

"Ohhh, ngg, th-that's so good," I mewl, my eyes threatening to cross from the pleasure overtaking me.

"Look how fucking greedy your cunt is, baby. You see how badly it wants my cock? It's practically begging for me to fuck it." He spits the words through gritted teeth, his body coiled with tension, veins pulsating throughout his arms and hands. "Is that what you want, Molly? For your little pussy to be fucked?"

I nod jerkily, attempting to utter a simple *yes*, but only managing to let out a sharp, slurred sound. I'm drugged on euphoria, yet I need more. I'm a fiend for it, and it's something only Cage can give me.

He drives completely inside me, and my eyes cross, while the most erotic whimper sounds from his throat.

"Oh— Fuck, Cage," I cry, the words as deprived of oxygen as my lungs.

His lips feather over my ear, and a deep foreboding gathers in my bones a moment before he gives his warning.

"Brace yourself, little ghost. I don't fuck kindly."

My heart rockets up into my throat, and I hurry to wrap my hands around his biceps, but he leaves me no time to prepare.

He retreats to the tip, and then he's driving into me, setting a hard, steady pace that steals my breath, my vision, my goddamn sanity.

Delicious moans spill past his lips, his pleasure as loud and unhinged as mine. It only drives the butterflies in my stomach wild, as if they have no direction to migrate, leaving them to wander.

"Fuck, Molly, your pussy is gripping me so tight," he groans. "You're clinging to me like a desperate little slut."

One arm unhooks from my leg before he slides his palm up my throat to cup the underside of my jaw. He grips tight, forcing my unfocused gaze to his. The emotion in his stare is just as intense as the way he pumps into me. It borders on obsession and has the organs in my body plummeting to the pit of my stomach.

"Eyes on me while I claim you," he growls. "I need you to see me like I see you."

"I see you," I whimper, though my focus is unstable.

I'm already nearing another orgasm, and I don't know that either of us will be able to contain my reaction when it hits.

There's no control over a natural disaster. Only allowing it to wreak havoc and bracing yourself for the outcome. The storm building inside me is catastrophic. It'll be devastating, and I'll be in ruins.

"Fuck, I'm going to come," I gasp, my eyes beginning to roll. I feel entirely out of control as I pummel toward that edge. My surroundings blur, and the only thing I can see through my fuzzy vision is his devilish grin. It looks like he's laughing at me, as if he's amused by how easily he can make me come. It's almost degrading, yet it sets me on fire anyway.

His hips pause suddenly, and immediately my orgasm wanes, a downward roll on a steep hill.

A frustrated groan is the only response I'm capable of.

"Didn't I already tell you to keep your eyes on me? I'm in the business of making you disappear, not in repeating myself," he states, his tone almost threatening. My glazed stare flies to his.

"I'm sorry, please keep fucking me," I rush out, rolling my hips to reignite the pleasure.

"Don't make me ask again, Molly," he murmurs before pinching my jaw harder, ensuring my attention stays locked on him.

I'm nodding, prepared to do anything he asks of me if it means he makes me feel good again.

"That's a good girl," he purrs darkly, finally resuming. Except this time, he angles his hips differently, hitting a spot deep inside of me that's never been reached before.

It's almost impossible to keep my eyes straight, but the expression on his beautiful face is as striking as it is heart-dropping. His mouth is parted as sexy moans pour from his tongue, and his thick brows are slashed above his eyes in an expression of ecstasy.

It takes no time to reach that pinnacle again and then go free diving off it.

His name rips past my lips in a scream that leaves my throat raw. Though, I'm unsure if I'd notice anything outside of the orgasm that crashes through me. It sends my back arching off the bed as if possessed by a soul-eating demon that's determined to leave everything in its path decimated.

The power of it is breathtaking, and whatever control I had over my body ceases to exist. My teeth rattle from how hard I seize, and my death grip on Cage's arms can't even keep me grounded.

There is no mercy in the way he continues to pound into me while spitting his own curses.

"I think you can do better than that," he bites out through clenched teeth.

I shake my head, delirious from the continuous onslaught of his thrusts yet understanding that he has no intention of stopping.

"I can't... I can't take any more," I pant breathlessly. "Please, it's too much!"

"Is it?" His tone is mocking, followed by a coo that suggests *'you poor baby.'*

My head kicks back, so entirely overwhelmed with the sensations that my brain is unable to compute how to handle it. I shift between trembling violently, slapping Cage's arms, to clawing at his flesh with little reserve.

"Let's see how tight that pussy can hold on to me," he growls. "Show me how a dirty little slut milks my cock."

"Fuck you," I choke out, starbursts beginning to explode behind my pinched eyes.

"You are, baby, and fuck, you're doing such a good job," he whimpers in my ear before drawing my lobe in his mouth and sucking.

A sharp outcry is the only sound I'm capable of uttering. A third orgasm takes hold of me, sending my soul into space where I float above and watch myself come wholly undone, my inner walls contracting around his cock.

"Fuuuuck, baby, that's it. Just like that, fuck yes, just like that. You're such a good girl," Cage chants against me.

His back muscles flex, and his thrusts become choppy, losing himself in time and space along with me.

"Molly," he rasps out, followed by a moan that is long and unrestrained. Distinctly, I feel him erupt, though I have the misfortune of the condom preventing me from feeling it inside me.

He stills, panting against my lips now, his breath syncing with mine. We're both shaking, and he relaxes on top of me, though he's careful to keep his weight from crushing me.

We're both silent for several minutes, spending the time searching for our breaths.

"I've been called a slut a lot," I admit after a few more moments, my voice cracking. He lifts his bowed head to gaze down at me carefully, waiting for me to collect my thoughts. "But I liked it when you said it. Just... only during sex, though, okay?"

He brushes a few strands away from my face gently.

"If a man ever calls you something you don't like, I'll fucking kill him. I'll always respect your boundaries."

I catch my bottom lip between my teeth before it can tremble. It takes a moment as the urge to cry subsides.

I've never felt so... respected. Like my feelings about what happens to my body are actually valued. Like they *mean* something to him.

"You're different," I mumble. "Thank you for showing me how to enjoy something I never thought I'd enjoy. For respecting my body. And for giving me something to hold on to before I disappear."

His eyes soften. "You can always hold on to me, Molly. Always."

chapter eighteen

MOLLY

PRESENT
2022

"I CAN'T DO A delivery today," I tell Legion, attempting to keep my nerves in check. I've never told him no before.

But this is necessary.

There's a pause. "May I ask why?"

I chew my bottom lip, contemplating if I should just tell the truth or not. However, I don't want my personal issues to come between me and my job. Or at least, I don't wish for Legion to know that.

"I'm uncomfortable with Cage," I blurt out.

That wasn't what I was planning to say. I was supposed to tell him my pigs are sick. Although it's technically the truth, though not in the way Legion is probably thinking.

I'm not uncomfortable because I don't like Cage; I'm uncomfortable because I like him way too much.

More silence.

After a few beats, I can't take it anymore. "I don't know if anyone has ever told you this, but your silence is super unnerving."

I'm sweating. It's forming along my hairline and between my boobs. I shake out my free hand to release some tension. I don't even know *why* I'm so nervous. Legion's never made me feel threatened. But *fuck,* he's really intimidating for a dude that never shows his face.

"What has he done?"

"Nothing!" I exclaim. "Don't kill him, please."

"Is this because he's in love with you? Or because you're in love with him?"

I slap my hand over my face. None of this is going to plan.

"That... No, neither," I stutter.

"Are you lying?"

"Legion," I groan. "I just think it's best that Cage and I no longer work together. That's all. Nothing personal."

It's *so* personal. I am such a liar—and not even a good one.

"Where's Eli? Isn't it time for him to come back?" I ask.

One Mississippi. Two Mississippi. Three Mississippi...

"Eli will do the delivery tonight. Your comfort is my priority."

My shoulders slump in relief. "Thank you, Legion."

"Have a good night, Molly."

The phone clicks off, and I instantly feel sick to my stomach. Legion will call Cage and tell him he's off the job. Maybe it'll be casual, and he'll tell Cage that Eli is simply ready to come back.

Or maybe he'll tell the truth, and Cage will come here demanding answers.

Which is something I'm not prepared for.

What the fuck am I supposed to say? That spending time with his mom and laying in his sister's bed listening to her favorite song scared the absolute shit out of me?

It only proves how much of a runner I am. How, even after all these years, I live like there's a target on my back. And, because of that, I refuse to let anyone get close.

I know that no one's coming after me anymore. Not really. According to Legion, Francesca and Rocco are dead, and Z destroyed the Society—which turned out to be some shadow government that was playing a massive hand in human trafficking operations.

Even if I were discovered by the public, I could easily lie and say I didn't make it out until years after my father and Layla's disappearance. No one could prove otherwise. But I've found comfort in my anonymity, and somehow, I've convinced myself that Cage is a threat to that.

I should've never agreed to dinner with his mom.

But it doesn't matter now.

I'm comfortable with my life. I've found my own retribution for what happened to me, and I don't need a man's love or his cock to fix me. I've already picked up every little, fucking, chipped piece of me and meticulously put them back together. I'm not broken anymore; I just don't work the same. But there's nothing wrong with being different.

I'm better off alone.

Francesca and her hound dogs made sure of that.

"Miss my face, huh? I always knew you couldn't resist me."

Eli's always been a nuisance in a sort of endearing way. But he's a loyal employee of Legion, and despite his terrible pickup lines, his jokes are harmless, and he's never made me uncomfortable.

I've been working with him since returning to Montana, and I have a soft spot for him.

"How could I? You're the full package," I answer dryly, though a small grin curls one corner of my lips.

He drops the dead body on my metal table, then splays out his arms as if he's presenting himself as a prize.

He's a cute guy—still in his mid-twenties with pretty brown eyes, a clean-shaven face, and a killer smile, though he's self-conscious of the front tooth that's slightly shifted over the other. His light brown hair is cut short and styled away from his face with probably five different products. He's one of those guys that takes his hair *very* seriously.

With how often he carries bodies around, he's lanky but fit, and he ensures to wear clothing that shows off just how many muscles he possesses.

Regardless, he's not my type. It seems only one man fits in that category, and it's always been Cage.

"I won't make you beg anymore. Come to papa."

I roll my eyes and grab my hair clippers, even though the old man has barely any left.

"Don't make me throw up on the corpse. I don't think my pigs would appreciate it."

He scoffs, and his upper lip curls in distaste. "Somehow, I think they'd consider it extra seasoning."

"Okay, that's disgusting," I mumble, faking a gag. I'm used to the filth that comes along with owning pigs. They're dirty animals, regardless of how hard I work to keep this place clean. Not just from blood but their grime, too.

And despite what I feed them for dinner, I still don't like to consider all the different things they'll eat. It's nearly limitless, and that in itself is rather unsettling.

"If I die, please don't feed me to them. Especially Oregano. That one is *too* eager when she eats," he pleas dramatically.

I snort, finishing shaving the dead man's hair and moving on to extracting his teeth. "Deal, as long as you don't let me become pig food, either."

He places a hand over his heart, like a soldier pledging his allegiance to the flag. "You have my word."

So dramatic.

"So what did this guy do?" I ask, nodding toward the corpse.

"Got a bit too friendly with his daughter. Most fucked-up part was that his friend was *also* assaulting her, and the dad pinned it all on him, and got away with it."

I shake my head, my heart hurting for the little girl. Oftentimes, I wish they brought these assholes to me alive.

"Have you spoken to Legion lately?" he asks, quickly changing the subject. The amusement on his face relaxes, settling his features into a more serious expression.

"I did earlier. Why?" I toss the teeth into the grinder and flip it on, the loud noise doing little to cut the building tension in the air.

"Did he mention anything about some brotherhood?"

My brows furrow as I remove the man's clothes. "Brotherhood?" I echo with confusion. "Doesn't sound familiar."

"Yeah, they're dubbed the Basilisk Brotherhood. Apparently, Z knows them now, and they're interested in your job in particular."

My hands freeze, and my muscles grow dense with tension. "What do they want with my job?" I ask, my voice hardening.

If they try to replace me... I'm going to throw a colossal fit. I get paid substantially to do what I do, and it doesn't require me to get any more involved in Legion's work than I want to.

I live a simple life, and I'm *happy* with that.

"They want the organs. Evidently, they think feeding them to pigs is a waste of money."

Now, my brows shoot up my forehead. When I meet Eli's stare, he explains, "They're organ traffickers. And I think they want to work with you and Legion."

I blink, having no idea what to think or feel.

"How come Legion told you about this and not me?"

"He asked me to meet with them first, get a feel for them before Legion entertains their offer. I'm sure he won't approach you about it until he's confident they're good people."

'Good people' is a loose term when it comes to this corner of the world. However, there's a surprising number of people like me. What we do wouldn't exactly grant us access to the pearly gates up above, even though we do it for good reasons. The ones we kill—even the devil wouldn't want them.

"If *Z's* working with them, then they must not be too bad," I comment, resuming my work and switching on the Sawzall.

Eli shrugs. "My thoughts as well, but you can never be too sure. I'd expect some type of contact regarding this soon. You might be making new friends."

I sigh, cutting off the man's head. Eli takes a step back when the blood splatters too close for comfort.

"Great. Just when I was getting used to you."

Eli gasps. "I resent that. Who else is going to tell you how sexy you are on a weekly basis?"

I raise a brow, unimpressed. "Somehow, I think I'll survive."

chapter nineteen

CAGE

TWO WEEKS LATER
2022

I CALL HER A little ghost, yet for some reason, I never considered that the brat would actually ghost *me*.

My blood simmers as I watch her from the depths of the woods surrounding her barn. As usual, the double doors are wide open, allowing the barn to air out. It's beginning to rain, the cold droplets doing little to cool my temper.

She's cleaning up after feeding her pigs, having just hung up the phone with the lady who confirms the corpses are disposed of.

She's meticulous. Has a routine that she doesn't stray from. And everything has a place.

Except for me, apparently.

A couple of weeks ago, Legion called to inform me Eli was back on the job, but immediately, I knew something was off when he not-so-kindly told me to forget where Molly lives and stay away unless she contacts me herself.

That was all I needed to hear to recognize that she was running.

It shouldn't have surprised me. Yet, it did.

More than that, it fucking *hurt.*

And it absolutely enraged me.

I have no doubts that Molly returns my feelings, except she's completely fucking clueless when it comes to being able to handle those emotions.

She may not have ever been in love, but she also has never met another like me.

And what she seems to forget is that I will *never* give up on her.

I've left her alone for two weeks, sticking to the shadows nearly every night since I got that call. Just observing her go through the motions of life as if I'm not the one who gives it to her. Waiting to see if she'd crack and reach out to me.

She hasn't, and my patience has waned.

God, how tempting it is to walk up behind her, wrap my hands around that dainty little throat, and show her that the only reason she can breathe is because I fucking allow her to.

"Fuck, you really piss me off," I bite out beneath my breath. I plunge my hand into my pocket and pull out my pack of gum, popping two pieces in my mouth this time.

I wait until she's finished at the barn, clicking off the overhead lights before making her way out into the trickling rain. She's not carrying the bag of clothes and hair that she typically burns when she's finished, likely due to the rain. Which means she'll probably wait to scatter the teeth in the mountains.

I contemplate leaving her be for another night. But that lasts all of half a second. My control snaps.

Legion will have to come out of hiding if he wants to try and stop me.

Two weeks without being able to inhale a full breath is torture enough.

Quietly, I make my way through the tall grass, keeping to the shadows as I approach her from behind.

She doesn't sense me until it's too late—her instincts having lightened over the past nine years.

She freezes, her shoulders stiffening and hiking to her ears, the panic snapping her spine straight. And then her damp, thick curls are fisted in my hand and I'm jerking her against my chest, my lips at her ear.

"For a little ghost with so many bones, you're just begging for me to break them," I growl.

A sharp gasp breaks through the melodic pattering of rain, and a shiver races down her spine so violently I feel it through her skin.

"Cage," she breathes, the pulse in her neck beating erratically. I'm tempted to press my teeth against it to taste something sweeter than the bitterness coating my tongue.

"What are you doing here?" she chokes out, resisting my hold. But I've let her pull away from me for long enough. She's lucky I don't sew her goddamn flesh to my own.

"Didn't I already tell you that I let you disappear on me once and I'm not going to allow it a second time? Did you think I'd just let you go so easily?"

"Yes," she squeaks when I fist her hair tighter, gritting my teeth as my fury renews. Just when I think I've calmed, I'm reminded that she actually tried to ghost me.

No proper explanation. No phone call telling me she doesn't want to see me again. Not even a fucking shitty breakup text. Just... silence.

"Then I suppose I haven't made myself clear enough. Allow me to remedy that."

"Cage, stop it!" she snaps, digging her heels into the wet grass when I shove her toward her house.

When she continues to fight, I scoop her up and throw her over my shoulder with a frustrated snarl.

"Walk away from me one more fucking time, Molly, and I'll make sure you can't walk at all."

"Don't you dare threaten me, asshole," she snaps.

While she sends her little fists flying into my back, I send the flat of my palm directly onto her plump ass.

"You dick!" she screeches as the loud slap reverberates into the cool night air.

A dark laugh unleashes from my throat, my muscles tightening with the need to punish her.

"Seems to me that's exactly what you need right now."

She huffs out an affronted sound and sends a hand diving into the back of my jeans to grab ahold of the waistband of my briefs, her threat clear.

I narrow my eyes as I climb her wooden porch steps.

"I'd just love to know what you think that's going to accomplish. If it's anything other than my cock shoved down your throat, you're sadly mistaken."

"You won't have a cock if I pull hard enough and cut off the circulation."

Completely unrealistic, but I let her have her little tantrum while I carry her into her house. All the while, she continues to threaten me, likely growing angrier by my lack of concern over a possible atomic wedgie. It'd probably hurt—would *definitely* piss me off—but it wouldn't make me drop her like she's hoping for.

She's made me into this, and now she has to fucking live with it.

"Cage, I swear to God, if you don't let me go, I will call Legion—"

"Don't make me find that faceless fucker and kill him," I snap. "He may have saved you before, but he sure as fuck can't save you now."

She growls at me, pounding on my back again. "Just let me go, and then we can talk like mature fucking adults!"

"Oh no, baby, you had that chance when you decided to run away rather than fall in love with me. Now, we do it my way."

She sputters for a moment, astonished. "Fall in lo—what are you talking about, you psycho? Just let me go!"

I smack my palm against her ass a second time, evoking another sharp gasp, but that was only a warning this time. Next, I slip my thumb between her clenched thighs and firmly press where her clit is.

She goes completely still.

"Stop it. Right now." Her voice is shaky, and those words are standing on grounds being ripped apart by an earthquake. But it isn't fear saturating her tone like she'd have me believe. The heat between her legs and nails digging into my leather jacket gives her true feelings away.

I can't help but smirk, rubbing tight little circles through her jeans as I head down the hallway directly ahead and toward her bedroom at the very end.

Little stuttered breaths sneak past her lips, though she tries to contain them, only for her throat to betray her and make a sound of its own.

She can't escape the pleasure any more than she can escape me. If I allowed it, she'd sooner rip her heart from my chest to steal it back, but unfortunately for her, she doesn't even realize I have it yet.

And I would never let her take away something so fucking precious.

But fuck, there's no denying that it's fun when she tries.

I toe open her door, revealing her bed with an olive green duvet, more distressed furniture, and artful pieces hung on the cream walls.

Standing at the end of her bed, I slide her down my body until I have her legs hooked around my hips.

She's glaring at me with glittering uncut emeralds, polished until her frustration is evident. Her bottom lip is slightly pouted, and her freckled cheeks are reddened with anger, brightening the white teeth imprint below her right eye.

She may be ferocious, but she's not very intimidating when she's cradled in my arms and my palms are cupping her ass.

"You're so goddamn beautiful," I murmur, completely enraptured by this woman. Christ, the things I'd do for her *and* to her. It's fucking limitless.

"You're being incredibly disrespectful right now," she snips.

My stare drifts to those plump lips that are just begging for me to bite them. "I haven't even begun to disrespect you yet, baby. But my God, how I look forward to it."

Her eyes narrow into thin slits, though her cheeks flush brighter.

"We can't be together, Cage," she states firmly, but once again, her words are brittle.

"Why's that?" I ask casually, still studying every inch of her face.

"B-because! I said so! I'm better off alone."

I offer my dry gaze for all of two seconds, ensuring she can see just how weak of an excuse that was.

We both know she doesn't have a truly good reason other than her being scared.

She huffs. "Maybe I just don't want a relationship. Is that not a valid enough reason? Do my feelings not matter?"

She's glancing away, unable to keep her stare hooked to mine now.

Running. She's running as we fucking speak. And that irritates me.

It's my turn to narrow my eyes, a disgruntled growl building in my chest. Instead of answering, I toe off my boots and climb onto the bed, dropping her flat on her back with a startled exhale.

She attempts to scramble away, but I've already anticipated her move and have her wrists pinned above her head before she can make it two inches.

Stray curls fall over her face, and she pants from below me, seething at me with a fire that rivals the heat emanating from her pretty little cunt.

"You're scared, and I get that. You've been alone nearly your entire life and don't know what it feels like to have someone take care of you. Fine, we can work through that." Then, I lower my voice, ensuring she can see just how fucking serious I am. "But what I will not do is allow you to run from me."

I lean down until my lips are a hairsbreadth away from hers, her breath warming my face in short bursts.

"Don't worry, little ghost. I'm going to teach you how to spend forever with me."

She blinks up at me with widened eyes filled with bewilderment.

"You're crazy," she breathes.

"About you," I correct. "I'm crazy about you."

"You barely know me."

"I know you better than you know yourself," I retort, my stare drifting back down to her pink mouth. "I don't need to know your favorite color to know that I was the first man to make you feel good in your own body."

That pouty bottom lip curls between her straight teeth, and I can't help the burn of jealousy. *I* want to bite it.

"Do you think it's better for me to know if you prefer bacon over sausage in the morning or that you've fought like fucking hell to get to where you are and would eat both just because you can?"

She cocks a brow. "You think I eat pigs for breakfast?"

The corners of my lips tip up, and my voice drops into a whisper. "I think you'd eat it right in front of them because you enjoy the morbidity of it just as much as chopping up dead people as their food."

"I think you're searching for things to love, but eventually, you're going to realize that I was never meant to be happy, and you're only wasting your time."

My chest tightens at the sorrow in her eyes, and the burning desire to fix it is insatiable. I will never know peace for as long as Molly Devereaux is sad.

"You can't fix me," she finishes.

"I don't want to fix *you*, Molly. There's nothing to mend when you've already done that yourself. The only thing I will do is ensure there isn't a single part of you that is empty. Your life, your heart, and your sweet pussy." I lean in closer until my lips lightly rest against hers. "Filling you will never be a waste of my time."

I'm crushing my mouth to hers before she can respond. She doesn't need to when her body is already doing so. Her back arches, pressing her chest against mine, and her lips part easily beneath the pressure of my tongue.

A little moan brushes the roof of my mouth, and it's the only confirmation I need that while she may run again, she sure as fuck loves being caught.

I pull away, catching her heavy-lidded stare. "Tell me that you're mine."

Her brows furrow, a small frown tipping down her swollen lips. "Since walking into your store, I don't think there was ever a time that I wasn't, Cage."

chapter twenty

MOLLY

THREE MONTHS LATER
2022

"GO EMMA!"

The scream comes from her mother, Margot, her blonde ponytail bouncing as she jumps up and down on the bleachers only a few rows from Cage and me.

I'm on my feet, screaming along with Margot, though I'm still careful not to say her name. Cage is also on his feet, clapping his hands loudly and wearing a smile on his face.

He doesn't know her, but he knows everything about her, and he's learned to care for her from afar, too.

There've been many sleepless nights where I cried for the little sister I'll never get to know, and he's held me every time, talking me through those moments until I reminded myself that she's happy.

"Are you going to introduce yourself to her?" Cage asks quietly.

My smile slips, and I shrug, trying to hide how the mere thought makes me want to vomit.

Cage took it upon himself to look deeper into Layla's life, just to ensure she was as happy as it seems on the outside. And she is. But he discovered that there might be a part of her missing, too. He found her posting questions on public forums anonymously, asking for advice about the possibility of her parents lying to her about her early childhood. She wrote that she has vague memories of another mother-like figure in her life, but her parents will tell her nothing about it. She knows she's adopted but feels like her parents are strangely secretive about where she came from and how they came about adopting her.

It broke my heart and made me question if I was genuinely doing the right thing by staying out of her life.

"I don't want her to know what I do," I say. Something I've said a million times before. "And I don't want to lie to her, either. She's been lied to enough in her life."

"Is one lie worth never knowing her at all?" he asks. Something he's asked a million times before.

And I still don't have a good answer.

He stares at me intently, and I'm reminded that he could only know his sister for twelve years. The choice to know her longer was taken away from him.

Guilt eats at me, and a battle rages inside my head, only I still haven't figured out who's winning. The part of me that wants to know her, or the part of me that feels she's better off without me.

Either way, Cage feels I'm taking that choice away from her.

"Her parents would hate me if I reappeared in her life, I think," I continue.

"Possibly. But only because they'll feel threatened. Maybe confused. But if you trust them with who you are, they might learn to trust you. You're not there to take Layla away from them."

"I would never," I agree. "She belongs with her family, and I'd never do anything to change that."

"You're her family, too, baby. And once they know that you're not trying to take her away, they might be happy to have you fill in those gaps for Layla. They're so secretive about her past because they don't *know*. They know nothing about who she really is or where she comes from, and maybe it'll bring them some peace, too."

It's all hypothetical.

Theoretical.

There's no way to know if that's how they truly feel, or if that's what they'd truly want. No way to know if it's even what Layla would want.

Sure, she might think she does. But what happens if I tell her, and it sends her into a tailspin because now she must face the fact that her birth parents were sick, depraved people? Would it cause an identity crisis? Would she feel like her blood is tainted by evil?

They're thoughts I've had to come to terms with myself. Would I end up like my parents eventually?

I don't want Layla to suffer from those insidious thoughts. I don't want her to ever know the pain of having her biological parents see her as nothing more than a cash cow. To know that she meant so fucking little to them.

Because she meant everything to me.

Everything.

Layla scores one more goal before the clock runs out, knocking the ball into the net with her head. Her team beelines for her, lifting her up in their arms and screaming for yet another win. They're undefeated so far, and it looks like they're quickly on their way to Nationals.

My heart bursts from pride, and I scream along with the rest of the team and their families, my hands stinging from how hard I clap them.

"Emma, Emma, Emma, Emma," the team chants, lifting her up on their shoulders. Yet, her head is swiveling to look back at the other team, their shoulders slumped. Despondence polluting the air around them. There's a slight frown on her face, almost as if she feels guilty for beating them.

It's all I need to see to know that she will *never* be like our parents.

I just hope that if I do meet her, she'll see that, too.

My heart is pounding in my throat, and I'm just wondering at what point my body decided it would function better there instead of my chest.

It's clearly gone rogue, along with any coherent thought as Layla and her parents approach.

Cage and I are standing outside the field gate, where throngs of people spill out as everyone leaves for the night. The warm August air is suffocating, and I wish I had brought a mini fan to keep me from sweating through all my clothes.

I doubt being a sopping mess will make an excellent first impression.

Layla and her parents emerge from the doors, her blonde strands matted to her sweaty forehead and a bright smile on her face as her dad, Colin, shakes her shoulders with excitement. Her head tips down, and that grin slips ever so slightly.

It's very little encouragement, considering I'm point two seconds from bailing, but it's enough to keep my feet planted until Layla is only a few feet away.

The world tilts on its axis, slowing to a halt as our eyes clash. I'm not sure if we're moving in slow motion or if she really has stopped walking. Regardless, there she stands, two feet away, and staring right at me.

"Emma?"

Layla's head snaps to Margot, who is staring at her with concern, her gaze darting between her daughter and me.

"You okay?"

"Uh," she stutters, but then refocuses on me before she can muster a better response.

"Emma, who is that?" Colin asks.

I bite my lip, my brain rolling over how to introduce myself. My real name? My fake name? Her sister? Does it even matter?

My mouth opens, then snaps shut, and I shift on my feet uncomfortably. This was a mistake. A huge mistake.

I have no place interfering in her life. Who cares if there's a small part of her missing? It's better than finding out your parents tried to sell you in the sex trade *after* they sold me.

That's like—*so* much trauma.

I go to turn, but Cage grabs my biceps, preventing me from running away.

"Who are you?" Margot is directing her question toward me now.

"Uh."

My response isn't any more informative than Layla's was, except I actually know the answer.

I clear my throat and try again, "Her sister."

All three of their spines snap straight, but while wariness and suspicion clouds over her parents' vision, Layla narrows her eyes in contemplation, as if she's trying to recognize me from memories almost a decade old.

"Excuse me?" Margot snaps, stepping forward, her tone sharp and irate. "What makes you thin—"

"I gave her to you," I say, my voice cracking. Fuck, it hurts so much to say it aloud, even if it was the best thing that I could've done for her. It just fucking sucks *I* couldn't be that. Cage's hand cups my bicep, gently squeezing to remind me he's here. It's enough to power on. "Ten years ago. I left her on your doorstep with a name tag and birthdate."

She and Colin blink at me in astonishment, a range of emotions flashing through their stares. I doubt they told anyone that; it certainly wasn't released to the public.

"You gave me away?" Layla asks, her voice soft and tinged with hurt. It's the first time I've heard it up close and directed at me. It's enough to move me to tears, though I manage to hold them back.

I chew on my lip, contemplating how to answer, only to settle on a shaky nod. I can't trust my voice not to crack and for a tsunami of an explanation to burst free. I know I need to take it slow with her—*if* she decides she wants to know me—but I hate that she feels like I abandoned her because I didn't want her.

"Why?" she asks.

"Maybe this isn't the best place for this to happen," Colin intervenes, glancing nervously between his wife and me. They're both on edge. Uncomfortable. And for good reason.

Maybe I should've sent her a message on some social media app instead, but that felt so... impersonal. Dirty.

I don't want Margot and Colin to feel like I'm sneaking behind their backs. Like some weird predator trying to gain Layla's trust without their knowledge.

I want to do this the right way. Maybe this wasn't the *best* way, but at least her parents won't be kept in the dark.

"You're right," I rush out. "I guess I didn't really know the best way to go about this—"

"You should've come to us first," Margot states firmly. She's aggravated, and her protective instincts are fully engaged. It's understandable, but keeping my voice even takes effort.

"Probably. But I didn't want to become a secret to her or a reason for you two to have to keep one if you tried to decide for her. I'm not here to try and take her away or cause any trouble. I chose you two for a reason, and I have no plans to undo that decision."

"Then what do you want?" Layla asks, cocking her head.

"To know you," I say, meeting her baby blue eyes. "That's all. If that's not what you want, I'll respect that. But I just wanted it to be you who decides."

Colin scoffs. "We get a say, too. She's only fifteen—"

"And she's going to grow up eventually," I remind him, my own tone sharpening. "She won't be fifteen forever. Just ask yourself if you'd be preventing her for her own sake or yours."

He looks slightly offended by that, but it doesn't make it any less accurate.

Swallowing back the bile threatening to spew from my throat, I take a few steps forward and hand Margot a piece of paper with my number written on it.

"Go home and talk about it as a family, yeah? Then call me when you all decide. I'll respect your decision regardless."

Hesitantly, she takes the slip from me. I spare Layla one last glance before turning and taking off.

"Hey!" Layla's voice stops me, and I turn enough to give her my eyes. "What's your name?"

I swallow, and for a brief moment, I consider giving her the name that I gave myself when I took her away from our awful home. But I want her to know the real me. The version of myself I've been fighting to find again since I became a ghost all those years ago.

"Molly," I rasp. "My name is Molly."

Then, I pivot and hope to God that this isn't the last time I'll ever hear her voice.

Cage entwines my hand with his, squeezing tightly.

"So, the little ghost finally materializes. Welcome to the rest of your life, baby."

epilogue

MOLLY

ONE MONTH LATER
2022

EVEN THE TIP OF Cage's dick in the back of my throat doesn't deter my thighs from seizing around his head. His tongue swipes through my slit, targeting my clit with perfect precision and skill.

I'm sitting on his face and leaning down his body, sucking on his cock until his own thighs tense with pleasure.

We're competing on who can make who come first. Whoever the winner is gets to fuck the other in the ass, and I'm determined to win. Yet, less than a minute in, and I'm on the verge of losing.

I take him down the back of my throat again, evoking a deep groan from his chest and causing him to pump his hips, forcing me to swallow him impossibly deeper.

I gag, but even that doesn't diminish the burning need to explode. Squeezing my eyes shut, I bob my mouth up and down his length with vigor, sucking and licking while using my hand to twist around the flesh that my mouth can't reach.

In retaliation, he sucks my clit into his mouth, flicking his tongue over it with a speed my brain is incapable of comprehending. The only thing it can grasp is how fucking amazing it feels.

My stomach tightens, and I reach that cliff within seconds. There's no stopping the orgasm rolling over me and off that edge, sending me flying off with it.

I scream around his cock, losing control of my body as I mercilessly grind into his face. His arms hook around my thighs, and he moans against me, opening his mouth to accept the eruption he so savagely forced out of me.

A few seconds later, he's filling my mouth, too. Hot ribbons of cum shoot down my throat, and the only thing I'm capable of is rolling my hips and swallowing him down until there's nothing left of either of us to give.

I pull back just as he does, the two of us panting for breath.

"Jesus fucking Christ," he breathes.

"What are you calling out to Him for? Clearly, He's on *your* side," I gripe without heat, rolling off him. "I was *this*—" I hold out my hand and pinch my forefinger and thumb a millimeter apart. "—close to getting to peg you."

He chuckles. "We got the rest of our lives. Let me work up to that, yeah? For now, I get to fuck your pretty little ass."

There's already a smug grin on his face as I lie down next to him, propping my chin on his heaving chest.

"Shut up," I say before he can start gloating. The smirk widens, and it's entirely unfair how beautiful it is.

"If it makes you feel any better, I had to pull out the big guns and think of some pretty fucked-up shit. I was ready to explode the second you deep-throated me."

I roll my eyes. "That means you cheated. I demand a redo."

"Deal," he agrees readily, the word rushing out of his mouth before I can barely finish.

I purse my lips, then smack his chest playfully. "You're just going to keep cheating, so I keep asking for a redo. Dickhead."

He laughs, causing my head to shake. Scoffing, I roll away from him, prompting him to roll after me and cocoon me in his arms, my back to his chest.

"You're right," he whispers sensually in my ear, eliciting a bone-deep shiver. "I'd do terrible, terrible things to get my mouth on that pussy as often as I can."

"I have one more body to grab," Cage says, only a little breathless after carrying in three dead men from Eli's trunk. Apparently, they were brothers and enjoyed sharing child porn with each other like they were goddamn cute puppy videos.

My brows pinch in confusion. "I thought Eli said he only dropped off three?"

"He did. I brought an extra."

I can only manage a blink before he's halfway out the door.

"What the hell?" I mutter, bewildered. The only response I receive is an obnoxious snort from Dill.

"What the hell?" I repeat a couple minutes later when he reappears, my tone louder and sharper.

My mouth drops as Cage carries in a very familiar man, dropping the body on the metal table. Someone that I only tend to see in my nightmares.

"Kenny Mathers," I whisper. The only man from Francesca's house who managed to get away unscathed and the last living man who abused me in that house. "How did you find out who he was? I never told you his name."

"Legion," he answers simply.

Of course. I should've known.

"How did you find him?"

"In a prison. Well—Legion's prison—not an official one. Keeping him locked up, away from society, until you made the initiative to kill him. I decided to do that part since you don't like to get involved in that side of the business."

"You killed him?" I repeat in a whisper.

"Sure did," he chirps proudly. "Legion handed him over to me, and I took care of the rest."

I stare at him, mouth agape as I try to process that not only did Legion keep my abuser locked away all this time, waiting for me to be ready, but that Cage killed him for me. And is now presenting him to me as... pig food.

"Wow," I choke out, completely overwhelmed. "I think I love you even more now, but I'm also not sure 'cause I didn't think that was even possible."

That's the first time I said those three words out loud, which is also a lot of emotions to deal with. Specifically as his eyes flare, and now he's watching me as if *I'm* the food.

"You got anyone else on that hit list of yours? I'll kill as many people as you want if you keep telling me you love me."

My vision is blurring, and my chest feels too full.

"You're an idiot," I croak, blinking away the tears. Cage grabs a hold of me and tugs me into his embrace, holding me tight.

"I'm going to fuck you for so long later tonight," he whispers sinfully.

I choke out a laugh, and he grabs my chin, bringing my focus to him. He stares at me softly, though there's a hint of that obsession still lingering in his eyes.

"I love you, too. Now, let's get to work chopping him up. Chili's giving me an evil eye, and Garlic and Paprika seem like they're conspiring against us as we speak."

The loud chirp of my phone ringing nearly causes my bones to climb right out of my flesh in fright.

I've had the sound up at full volume ever since I handed Margot my phone number; I've just been waiting for her to call.

It's been a little over a month, and I've all but convinced myself their silence is my answer.

Either Layla doesn't want to get to know me, or Margot and Colin won't allow her to. Regardless, it's not my place to interfere with either decision. Even if it feels like my heart is in tatters.

"You gonna get that?"

Cage and I are in the process of extracting teeth and buzzing hair off Kenny and the other three dead bodies.

I glance at the number, noting that it's one I don't recognize. Pulling my gloves off, I press the answer button and hold it to my ear.

"Hello?"

"Molly?"

My heart pauses for a beat. "Yeah?"

The woman clears her throat. "This is Margot. Emma's mom."

I nearly stumble over air as I whip around and begin to pace.

"It's so nice to hear from you," I choke out.

"How long have you been going to Emma's games?"

I frown, a little taken aback by the question.

God, what if she's calling just to tell me Layla said she doesn't want to know me? What if she tells me to never contact them again or show my face at any of her games?

I'll always go to her games but respect their wishes enough to not let them see me. I'll keep my distance for as long as Layla demands. If it's forever, I would be okay with watching her grow old from afar—as long as she's safe.

"I moved back to Montana over four years ago. As soon as I discovered that she was playing, I went to all her games. Every single one."

Margot is silent for a moment, and then I hear a soft sigh.

"Emma is... she's interested in talking to you," she begins, her voice taut with discomfort. "She admitted that she had been feeling a little lost about her early childhood and would like to know about her biological parents. And you, of course. We agreed only because we feel it would help Emma heal from... from her abandonment issues."

I close my eyes, feeling as if Margot is standing before me and tearing her claws into my flesh until my heart is exposed, then ripping it out of its useless cavity. No bones could ever protect it from Layla's hurt.

"I understand," I whisper. "I will tell her anything she wants to know."

"And I know who you are. Who she is," she rushes out, almost as if, if she didn't get it out she'd combust.

"I see. Then I hope you know that I didn't give Layla to you because I didn't want her, but because I had to."

There's silence, and it's only now that I notice Cage has shut off his own hair clippers. It's quiet—too quiet.

"Emma," she corrects. "Her name is Emma."

I bite my lip, not realizing I slipped up.

"I know it is," I concede softly. "I gave that name to her so no one would find out who she was."

"Right," Margot says, her tone curt but not lacking heat. I know this is hard for her as well.

"I appreciate you allowing me to speak to her. At least this once. I... I can't even begin to express how much she means to me."

Margot sighs again. "I believe you, Molly. I can't imagine the things you've been through. The things Emma has been through. If I'm being honest, I wasn't going to allow this when you first approached. But... once I googled you and found out about your story—your kidnapping—I realized there may be a lot more to both of your stories than I was giving credit for. In my head, I built you up as some drug-addict mother who left her kid on some random stranger's doorstep. I used to thank God every night that she was left with us and not someone who would've hurt her. I remember you said that you chose us. Is that true?"

"I did," I answer. "It's a little creepy when I say it out loud, but I watched your family for months. I couldn't leave her with just anyone, but I didn't trust the system, and I wanted her to go to a family that I knew would keep her and love her."

"Well, you chose correctly," Margot says. "So I will pay you the same respect and let you see her. But know that the moment Emma says she's done, you will *never* see her again. Is that understood? She is—"

"Your daughter," I assure. "And I understand. I will respect her wishes. Always, Margot."

She releases a heavy exhale, as if a small weight has been lifted from her shoulders.

"Okay. I will text you a date and time."

"Thank you," I breathe. The phone clicks off, and immediately, tears spring to my eyes and spill over in rivers as if they were poised at my lash line, waiting to be released.

"What happened?" Cage asks, rushing over to me and cupping my face between his palms. Thankfully, he had the foresight to take off his rubber gloves, even though his body is still covered in blood from extracting their teeth.

His eyes dart between mine, concern etched into his slanted brows.

"She's going to let me see Layla," I croak, the end of my declaration broken by a hiccup.

"Come here, baby," Cage mumbles, ushering me into his arms. I keep my chin tilted up and away from his chest, while he bows his forehead to rest on my shoulder, hugging me tightly.

The cap that was held tightly over the emotions I had bottled inside me during the conversation bursts off, and I lose myself, sobbing into his neck while he sways us side to side.

So much fear, hurt, and loneliness is released from my chest. Ten years without seeing her beautiful smile, hearing her say my name—it's been torture. Worse than anything I've ever suffered at the hands of dirty men.

I had never known love until Layla was born, and for years, my world revolved around her seeing another day. Then, it revolved around protecting her from me and all the baggage that I towed around.

And now, it feels like I've finally been set free. From the chains that were wrapped around my ankles, constantly dragging me back into my sordid past every time I tried to escape it.

"I get to see her," I squeak out between harsh wails.

"You get to see her. And she'll get to love you now."

That only makes me cry harder. I've never known a god, but if one exists, He'll grant me my sister's love. That's all I've ever wanted.

I'm not sure how much time passes before my cries die down, my throat raw, and my eyes bloodshot and swollen.

Cage pulls away just enough to swipe the tears from my cheeks with his thumbs.

"I love you, little ghost. And I know she will, too."

I hiccup as he leans in and rests his lips against my forehead, kissing me there softly.

"I love you, too."

Just as I catch my breath, my phone goes off again, and for a second time, scaring the absolute shit out of me.

Clearing away the lingering emotion from my throat, I answer without looking.

"Hello?"

"I hear you're good at making people disappear."

The deep, male voice is jarring and not what I was expecting. I pull the phone away from my ear, checking the number. It's unknown.

"Who is this?"

"Most know me by Z. But you can call me Zade."

THE END

MOLLY IS FIRST INTRODUCED IN THE CAT & MOUSE
DUET. IF YOU HAVEN'T ALREADY, PICK UP THESE
BOOKS TO EXPERIENCE ALL THIS WORLD HAS TO
OFFER!

READING ORDER:

SATAN'S AFFAIR
HAUNTING ADELINE
HUNTING ADELINE

also by h. d. carlton

H. D. CARLTON

acknowledgments

First as always, a huge thank you to my readers. You all have put up with my slow writing and stuck around during times of extreme burnout where I didn't know if I was successfully going to be able to write another book. I can't thank you enough for your continued support, and being someone I can rely on no matter what. I love you all from the depths of my black soul.

Secondly, thank you to my amazing husband. Without your support, I wouldn't be where I am today. We're the best power couple that ever lived, in my personal opinion. You're also the best husband in the world, and I'm so glad to be dominating the world with you by my side. I love you so much.

And thank you to Sam, the most dedicated stalker, and my best friend. You've been an incredible support system and looking at your face 24/7 while you yell at me to write while simultaneously distracting me with anal tattoo ideas has been the highlight of my days. Even if it was initially forced, I'm so thankful you're in my life. Forever. I love you, weirdo.

Kristie and Samantha, sitting in the diner with you two is one of my favorite memories. And where Molly's story was born. I love you both and am so eternally grateful for you two.

Next, thank you to my alpha readers, Amanda, May, and Tosh. I would trust all three of you with a trust fall, but even more, I can trust you guys with my book babies, and that's some real shit. Thank you for never being my yes-men, but always my biggest supporters. And thank you for tearing my books apart and treating me like a commoner that can barely spell, kicking my ass when I don't know the answers to questions about my own books, and figuring my shit out for me. My books definitely would not be what they are without you three.

To my betas, Autumn, Nicki, Ana, Janine, and Taylor, I appreciate all of you so damn much. Again, for not being my yes-men, but incredible supporters who kick my ass. Thank you, thank you, thank you for being by my side.

Thank you to my kick-ass editors, Angie and Rumi. Thank you for always making these books look shiny. I appreciate you both so much.

And last but certainly not least, thank you to my bestie, cover designer, and cheerleader, Cassie. You always make these covers so beautiful, but your soul is even prettier. I love you.

about the author

H. D. Carlton is a USA Today and International Bestselling Author. She lives in Ohio with her partner, two dogs, and cat. When she's not bathing in the tears of her readers, she's watching paranormal shows and wishing she was a mermaid. Her favorite characters are of the morally gray variety and believes that everyone should check their sanity at the door before diving into her stories.

Learn more about H. D. Carlton on . Join her newsletter to receive updates, teasers, giveaways, and special deals .
And if you're brave, join the for extra early torturing—I mean teasing.

Facebook
Twitter
Instagram
Goodreads

SO, YOU DECIDED TO STICK AROUND, HUH?
HERE'S YOUR REWARD...

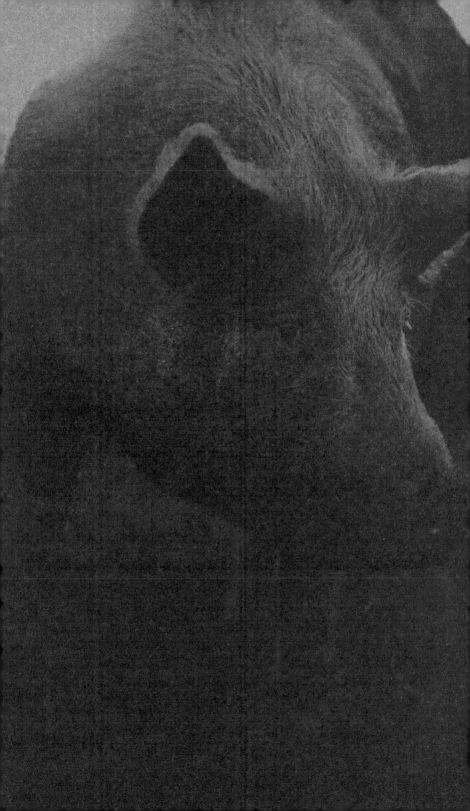

extended epilogue

MOLLY

PRESENT
SEPTEMBER 4ᵀᴴ, 2023

"JESUS *FUCK*, YOU'RE TALL," I breathe, my eyes rounding.

The man strides into my barn like he owns the place, and if he demanded it of me, I just might concede. Not only is he tall, but he's also fucking scary-looking.

The contrast between his dark brown eye and light blue eye is startling. And the scar cutting through the left one—starting from just above his eyebrow and straight down to the middle of his cheek—only heightens the savage look he possesses.

No wonder he's the head of the most prominent organization in the world.

Behind him walks in a considerably shorter woman, her long cinnamon brown hair fashioned into a loose braid over her shoulder.

I recognize her immediately. Not only as a famous author—whose books I fucking *love*—but the woman who was kidnapped and found herself in the clutches of Francesca, just as I was. When I heard Z found her, I nearly cried in relief that someone else had made it out of there, too.

She's beautiful and has some of the prettiest light brown eyes I've ever seen. And *definitely* is fucking the big boss, if the way Z—or rather, *Zade*—looks at her like he'll murder Cage and I in a heartbeat if we even so much as sneeze on her is any indication.

She's glancing around the barn, her mouth agape as she takes in my setup.

"Oh, Sibby would *love* this," she mutters to herself.

In response to my comment about Zade's height, Cage turns to me with a *what the fuck?* look on his face. "Baby, he's only, like, two inches taller than me." He points a thumb to his chest. "I'm tall, too."

I glance at Zade. "He's... scarier."

Cage's eyes droop with exasperation while Zade shoots me a charming grin, stretching the scar on his face.

"I only hurt people who deserve it. Scout's honor," he assures.

The woman rolls her eyes. "He was never in Boy Scouts. And he's scary, but I can kick his ass, and *I'm* nice." She rushes forward, holding out her hand for me to shake. "I'm Addie. His fiancée. Thank you so much for having us."

I shake her hand, appreciating that she has a firm grip. I never trust anyone who can't give a proper handshake.

She squeezes my palm tighter, her eyes sparkling with awe. "You will never understand the impact you've had on my life, and I've been wanting to meet you for so long."

I blink, bewildered.

"I found your old journal in Francesca's house," she explains. "The one you wrote in during your time there. It... Your words saved me in a way I can't even express. They helped me get through the days there. I started writing in it after you. I still journal even now, all because of you."

"Oh, my God," I breathe, still in utter shock. "You found it? I honestly had forgotten all about it..."

"That journal saved my life, Molly. *You* saved my life, in a way." She shows me her wrist, which is covered with a beautiful tattoo of roses trailing up her arm. "There used to be a barcode here, but I got it covered. It's really small, but in one of the petals, I added your name. I carried you with me in that house, so I wanted it to be permanent, too."

She points to one of the roses, and instantly, my hand covers my mouth, eyes welling with tears as I stare at the five small letters scribed expertly inside the petal.

When I was in that house, they hadn't tattooed us, but I could only imagine the new precautions they started taking after I successfully escaped. I never imagined tagging them like fucking animals would be one, and it breaks my heart. But I also never imagined my journal would save someone else, and for that, I'm so fucking thankful.

Dropping my hand from my mouth, I lift my watery eyes to her, gazing at her with a little sorrow, and a lot of pride. "You did that, Addie. *You* got out."

She gently grabs my hand and squeezes. "I did it with your help."

Entirely speechless, she leaves me to process that, moving on to Cage.

The only thing that brings me back to reality is Zade's sharp stare cutting to where their hands connect for point two seconds. He keeps quiet, but Jesus, he was definitely counting how long they touched for. I'd hate to find out what would happen to my boyfriend if it were a second too long.

I'd go down, though I'd sure as fuck go down fighting.

My brain is still lagging from Addie's proclamation, so it takes me a moment to absorb Zade's words.

"Scar buddies."

Again, I blink. "Scar buddies?"

His finger flicks between our faces. "We both got dope scars. You know what that means? We should be friends."

Again, I blink.

Zade grins at my bewilderment, and continues, "Legion tells me you're a valuable asset. Murdering people happens to be my second favorite thing in the world, following my fiancée, of course. I'd feed your pigs really fucking well, and I have no problem doubling your salary to work with *Z*."

I cock a brow, crossing my arms over my chest. "I'm loyal to Legion."

The grin that slices across Zade's face is quick. "I was hoping you'd say something so noble. It means you're a damn good employee. However, I respect Legion, and he's agreed to share. You'll still work with him, and Eli will continue to deliver the food. Your pigs and wallet will just get a little bit fatter, that's all."

Then his stare snaps to Cage. "I hear you're also valuable. I pay good money for skills like yours."

Cage cocks his head. "Can't you do what I do just as easily?"

Zade shrugs. "Sure. But I don't need the extra workload when I have your expertise. I sent a few people to your store so I could see your work, and I have no problem admitting I haven't seen it done better than you."

Cage's brows jump in surprise.

"You'd be valuable. You both would," Zade continues. His intense stare slides over us, probing and analytical, while Addie goes to coo at the pigs. "So, are the two of you down?"

Mine and Cage's stares cut to each other at the same time.

I'm not sure why, but it feels like Zade is going to introduce me to a whole different world. One that will bring me out of the reclusive shell I've been comfortable in for the past decade.

And I guess... I guess I'm finally ready for it.